BRENDA AULT
144 E. Olson
Midland, MI 48640
517-835-1803

THE KING'S
REWARD

GOD'S TOUGH GUYS

Stephen, *the First Martyr*
Samuel Kirkland, *Misionary to the Senecas*
St. Vincent de Paul, *Priest and Pirate Captive*
Eric Liddell, *Olympic Star*

GOD'S TOUGH GUYS

THE KING'S REWARD

A Story of Vincent de Paul

DENISE WILLIAMSON

Illustrated by JOE BODDY

WOLGEMUTH & HYATT PUBLISHERS, INC.
Brentwood, Tennessee

for my friends
at Zion Mennonite Church

THE KING'S REWARD
Text © 1991 by Denise J. Williamson
Illustrations © 1991 by March Media, Inc.

Wolgemuth & Hyatt, Publishers, Inc.
1749 Mallory Lane, Brentwood, Tennessee 37027

Book Development by March Media, Inc., Brentwood, Tennessee

First Edition June 1991

PRINTED IN THE UNITED STATES OF AMERICA

Library of Congress Cataloging-in-Publication Data

Williamson, Denise J., 1954–
    The king's reward : a story of Vincent de Paul / Denise Williamson.
— 1st ed.
        p.   cm.
    Summary: Antoine becomes page to the king and is able to free a
friend from the galley ships with the help of his friend Father
Vincent de Paul.
    ISBN 1-56121-059-5
    [1. Vincent de Paul, Saint, 1581–1660—Fiction.   2. France-
-Fiction.]   I. Title.
PZ7.W6714Ki   1991
[Fic]—dc20

                                                    91-11172
                                                        CIP
                                                        AC

CONTENTS

No one can serve two masters. Either he will hate the one and love the other, or he will be devoted to the one and despise the other. You cannot serve both God and Money.

—*Matthew 6:24*, NIV

1

THE RESCUE

The pirates left only one torch burning on the deck of French ship *Hirondelle*. With drawn swords the thieves forced her sailors to kneel in darkness. Just before dawn a sharp voice rang out from the poop deck at their backs. "I'm coming down, you lousy cowards. And be warned. If any man looks at me, I'll pluck out his eyes!"

Antoine de Romarin shivered as he pressed his chin to his chest. His body was aching. Now a new wave of fear sliced his breath. "It's the evil Turk Rodomonte who speaks," the old sailor beside him wheezed. "Indeed, he will spill blood carelessly. Whatever happens, lad, hold your tongue. I pray to God you will be saved."

Footsteps thumped on the stairway leading down from the stern. A pair of polished boots came close enough for Antoine to see them from the corner of his eye. "Your captain lies dead on his bunk," the pirate jeered. "But you can save your skins. Turn over Comte de Romarin's son, and the rest of you go free."

Antoine quaked. Comte de Romarin was his father!

"I know the owner's boy sails with this crew." One of

the cutthroat's black-toed boots tapped Antoine's knee. "And I'll find him myself, if your jaws lock." He kicked Antoine harder. "What might your name be?"

The curved blade of Turk Rodomonte's scimitar touched Antoine's chest. As he felt the pressure, there was a shuffling of shoes on deck. The pirate pulled back instantly. He jumped toward the sound. Unable to help himself, Antoine raised one eye. He saw a lanky sailor struggle to his feet. The blazing torch lighted a young man's face.

"Not you, Luc!" Antoine groaned inwardly. His sixteen-year-old brother dared to face this man!

"The Comte de Romarin is my father," Luc said with his eyes cast down. "Take me. Free my father's men."

In a flash the pirate tossed a rope around Luc's neck and pulled it tight. Antoine could not hold back his scream. "Don't touch him!"

The deck of the *Hirondelle* faded, and Antoine found himself sitting up in a wide soft bed.

"Antoine! Wake up!" A blond woman with wide, blue eyes stood beside him with a candle.

Rubbing his mouth, Antoine remembered where he was. "Oh, Madame de Gondi," he said, blinking into the tiny flame. "I must have been dreaming. Did I wake everyone?"

The two de Gondi boys, in nightshirts like his own, stared at him from their mother's side. Embarrassed, Antoine moved his eyes toward the tapestries on the castle wall. "Poor child, you must be ill," the woman fretted. "I will call for my doctor and my priest."

"Oh, don't!" Antoine begged. "It was just a dream."

"Then tell us about it!" The younger dark-eyed boy jumped up and down. "I love getting scared!"

"You do not, Jean!" His brother Henri gave a disgusted shake of his blond head. "And besides, boys as old as Antoine don't cry *because of dreams*. I think he's sick, Mama, maybe with some disease he caught from sailors on his father's ships."

"Stop this," Madame de Gondi said. "Doctor Renoir will know what's wrong. But until he can be called, I want both you boys to leave Antoine alone."

Petit Jean pouted but Henri grinned as they followed their mother to the door.

Angrily Antoine closed the dark drapes hanging around his bed and dropped his head to the pillows. Soon the door latch clicked and a circle of light spread on the curtain. He could hear someone quietly crossing the room.

"Antoine?" A man's soft voice spoke as the light stopped growing. "Antoine de Romarin, may I speak with you?"

Antoine bit his lip and kept silent.

The draperies parted slightly, and he saw the dark eyes and broad nose of a priest in a plain black cap and robe.

"Madame said you had a nightmare. I came to see if there's something I can do."

Antoine fought the lump growing in his throat. "It was just a dream. Why does she have to be so concerned?"

The priest's smile deepened the lines that marred his

wide forehead. "Ah, she's a mother hen to any chick who pokes his head under this roof. Please, do not think unkindly of her."

Antoine sank lower in the sheets.

"You are sure you are all right?" the priest asked, holding the lamp a little higher.

Antoine nodded, and as he did, the door opened again. Beyond the priest he saw his father.

"Excuse me. Monsieur Vincent?" the comte said with tense impatience. "I appreciate your getting out of bed to be here. No doubt, you know Madame well enough to know she can be excited by little things. I am sure nothing is wrong with Antoine. Still, I would like to see him alone."

"Certainly." The priest's robe touched his heels as he nodded respectfully to the taller and much more handsome man. "Outside heaven itself, a boy can find no better comfort than that of an understanding father." The comte smiled graciously at the homely, broad-shouldered clergyman. But as soon as the priest was gone he pounded his oil lamp down on the bedside table. "What did you tell him?"

"I said nothing, Father." Antoine lowered his eyes.

"You dreamed about Luc again, I suppose?"

"Yes." His voice weakened. "Madame sent the priest because she heard my cries."

"And she's calling a doctor, as well."

"I know, Father. I tried to stop her. I tried to tell her I wasn't sick."

"It would be better if you were sick." His father groaned as he rubbed a hand across the thin spot in his light brown hair. "There is some dignity in illness, Antoine. There is none in dreams."

"I know," he whispered. "You've told me that before."

His father traced the edges of his beard in silence. "Now perhaps you will believe me. Do you want the whole de Gondi family to see you as a simpleton or a coward?"

"Please forgive me, Father," Antoine hesitated. "But if you told General de Gondi why I dream, maybe he would understand. Since he commands all the Mediterranean galleys that guard the coast, wouldn't he know of Turk Rodomonte? You told him that I went to sea, but you never said what happened on the *Hirondelle*."

"And I will never speak of it!" his father returned hotly. "Thousands of French sailors are in Turkish hands. What would the general think of me if I came to his estate bemoaning the loss of one more French-born son?"

"Why did you come, then?" Antoine asked.

"To seek the king's protection for the cargo vessels I still have." The comte folded his arms across his white shirt. "I would speak to King Louis himself, if I could."

Antoine sighed.

"You know, you could be captain of a galley someday." Antoine's father's green eyes flashed. "Instead of crying about pirates, you could kill them. Since the days when you and Luc were very young, the general has continually promised positions for you. That is why I put you on the *Hirondelle*. You are twelve, and I wanted the general to know you have already had some contact with

11

the sea before we made our annual visit to Villepreux."

"After facing the pirates, Father, I want to spend my life in Romarin."

"And do what? Raise jasmine and roses like some low-ranking farmer? Antoine, I am not just a perfume merchant anymore. I am a nobleman now. When are you going to start acting like a nobleman's son?"

Antoine looked away. "I don't know."

"Be quiet," his father ordered suddenly. "Others are coming. I want to say you are asleep."

Reluctantly Antoine turned his face to the wall.

"Ahh, Madame de Gondi and my own dear Corinne," the comte said as Antoine heard the door open. "Speak softly. As you see, Antoine is resting."

"But the doctor is here." It was Madame de Gondi's voice.

"Docteur," the Comte said warmly, "thank you for coming. I seek your professional advice. We just arrived from Provence last night. Is it not possible for our boy to have one troubled night after such a tiresome journey?"

"Fatigue could cause such distress," the unfamiliar voice replied.

"Ahh, and say my Antoine suffers from such fatigue," the comte pressed on. "Is sleep not the best remedy?"

"That is wise." Antoine heard the doctor sigh. "Perhaps you would like me to come again later?"

"Very good!" There was triumph in the comte's voice. "Let's give him an entire morning's rest."

"But the hunt, Joseph." Antoine quietly rolled over to watch his pretty dark-haired mother through squinted eyes. "He will be so disappointed if you don't let him ride."

"You heard the doctor, my dear. There will be other days. After all we will be with the general almost a week. Please, Madame de Gondi, see that Antoine has privacy until noon."

Noon! Antoine hammered the mattress as soon as the door closed. His father had turned his bed into a prison. Left and right, he tossed while the June sun heated the room. Again he rolled, but this time he spotted two dark eyes looking at him from the edge of the bed.

"Jean, you are not supposed to be here." Antoine stripped back the drapery that hid the five-year-old.

"I know, but Mama has breakfast guests and my nanny fell asleep, so I can do what I want."

"But if your mother finds you—"

"—I will say that Nanny let me. She told me I could watch the king's hawks fly as long as I stayed indoors. And you have the best window. It looks out on the swamps."

"The *king* hunts with his falcons on your father's land?" Antoine said with disbelief. "I doubt that! He has estates of his own."

"I know," Jean said impatiently. "But he likes our land best! Here. I brought you a pastry, a peach, and some bread from breakfast. Now can I stay?"

Antoine shrugged as he took the food. He ate while the little boy opened the floor-length window. Then Jean pushed a heavy cloth-covered chair in front of it so he could sit and watch what happened outside. "If you're going to use that seat, watch out for my clothes," Antoine complained. "Put my doublet and breeches on the back of the chair."

Jean obeyed silently. "Aren't you going to watch?" he asked, bouncing on the cushioned seat. "I think I see one of the birds right now."

Antoine slid from the bed and walked across the marble floor in his stocking feet. He surveyed the huge marshland that gleamed like a tarnished mirror in the middle of the valley. "You are right! I see a white hawk against the sky. It's a gyrfalcon, for sure. They're so rare, I'd say it has to be a royal bird."

Jean giggled. "Of course, it's a royal bird. Any bird that belongs to the king is a royal bird."

Antoine rolled his eyes.

"Look now!" Jean squealed. "Did you see that splash when the falcon hit the water?"

"That's not good!" Antoine exclaimed, stripping off his nightshirt and pulling on his clothes.

"What are you doing?"

"I'm getting ready to go out there. She's landed a swan in deep water. I know something about falconry from watching it in Romarin, enough to fear that the king's bird might drown."

"But it's all mud and weeds," the little boy said excitedly. "Papa never lets us go that way."

Antoine, however, had already stepped beyond the window to a small walled patio. Hearing dogs bark, but seeing no riders, he felt he had to go. He climbed the wall, raced down the green lawn, and scraped through the prickly hedge into taller grass. He kept running until chin-high weeds and boggy ground forced him to slow down. The mud was up around his ankles before he saw the huge white bird again. She was out in the green water with her talons locked into a dead swan's breast. Half of the gyrfalcon's great body was in the water. Her beak gaped as she struggled for air.

Antoine stripped off his doublet and waded in up to his chest. The falcon's eyes widened as he touched her prey. He pulled the dead bird and the falcon that clung to it toward shore. But just as he reached land, two huge bony dogs lunged from the weeds. Antoine sucked in breath. The dogs' throats rattled. Their lips turned back, showing yellow teeth. He was trapped. For safety, he retreated into deeper water.

Raising one foot from the muck, he took off his shoe. It was a poor weapon against two dogs, but it was the only one he had. He raised the heel above his head. At that instant, gunfire cracked the air. One dog yelped in pain, and both of them raced away.

Antoine, sagging with relief, saw seven riders churn up the murky water as they raced along the brushy shore. The first man, dressed in the blue doublet of a royal guard, ran his black charger close enough for Antoine to feel the horse's body heat.

"The falcon's here!" The guard motioned with the pistol he had fired and reined his horse to drier ground. In response, a rider clothed in white raced his mare toward Antoine. The guards who followed stopped to watch anxiously as the man dismounted. Throwing his plumed hat to the weeds, he waded in until the water touched the upper fringes of his hipboots. As he reached

for the tangled birds, Antoine's hand slipped away. His eyes moved from the thick black hair and boyish face to the emblem of a cross and dove hanging from a ribbon at the man's chest.

"The king himself!' Antoine breathed as Louis the Thirteenth slipped a feather-topped hood over the hawk's eyes and brought both birds to shore. The falcon, calmed by her temporary blindness, dug her beak into the bloodied swan as soon as she was on the grass. The king watched with quiet satisfaction. His bird was safe and unafraid to eat.

Antoine, feeling like an intruder on the scene, slipped to shore and found his doublet. He started back to the de Gondi castle through the high weeds. But he had gone only a few paces when three more riders galloped up.

"Antoine!" As he heard his name he saw his father rise in his saddle. The general and Henri were at his side. "What are you doing? Look at you! A mess!"

But the general caught Antoine's father by the arm. "Quiet!" he ordered. "The king is here. Dismount, with hat in hand."

Everyone bowed as the king walked past with the great bird on his wrist. The general then followed Louis the Thirteenth to his mare. "Sire, I heard a shot. I left my own hunting party to see if something might be wrong."

"Yes, General." The king paused in front of his stirrup. "If it had not been for a boy's quick thinking, my gryfalcon might be dead."

"My son saved the king's bird!" The comte threw a hand across his heart. "It is too good to be true!"

The king spied Antoine's father kneeling in the mud. "Where is your son now?" he asked.

Antoine found the courage to come out of the weeds.

The general smiled. "This is Antoine de Romarin, Comte de Romarin's son." Though he had never been in the presence of royalty, Antoine felt it would be right to bend down on one knee. "His father and I are childhood friends," the general went on. "I look forward to the day when I can assign this young man to one of Your Majesty's ships."

"A worthy plan," the king replied. "Even so, I wish to give him a reward now. Antoine, what is your request?"

"O-Ohh, to see your gyrfalcon and to have a part in saving her—that is enough for me," Antoine stammered.

"*Ma foi!* The boy has manners and courage! With enough youngsters like him at court I could raise an army of generals in ten years. But come, Antoine, surely there is something you would like."

"I-I know my father longs to speak with you." Antoine paused. "C-Could this be my request?"

Lifting his eyes cautiously, he saw the king rub his bare chin. "Comte de Romarin, have the general bring you to my chambers in the palace—tomorrow morning at eight."

"We will be there, Sire." The general bowed, then went to his horse.

"Your Majesty, you are too kind," the comte added, pulling at his hat in his hands.

"It was your son who was kind," the king observed.

"Since he asked a favor for you, I will let you make one request that will benefit him."

"Ahh, Sire, nothing could benefit him more than a small place of service in your court. I would not even think of mentioning it, except that you yourself said favorable things regarding his actions and his words."

"I will make him a page," the king replied easily as Antoine's eyes expanded in wild surprise. "It will be excellent preparation for a career at sea."

Antoine's father doubled over in gratitude. "Thank you. Thank you. A thousand times over, you deserve the name 'Louis the Just'."

The king looked at Antoine. "I am going to Paris by way of my country estate. With your father's permission I could take you now. Then at Saint-Germain you may pick a mount from the royal stable as a gift from me. Every page must have a horse."

"Father, what do you say?" Antoine gasped in amazement.

"Splendid! Go!" The edges of the comte's smile were lost in his trim beard. "Serve our king! Serve him well!"

"Then, Antoine, rise," the king said.

The guard on the black horse rode forward a few steps. "Your Majesty, you have the bird. I will be glad to take the boy with me."

"Very good, Lieutenant. Give him your hand."

Numbed by the sudden happenings, Antoine raised his arm, put a foot in the guard's freed stirrup, and felt himself being lifted up to sit behind the saddle.

As he looked for his father, he saw Henri carrying the

king's plumed hat. "I believe this is yours, Sire," Henri said with a bow.

"Ahh, my young Henri. Shall I make you a page, too?" The king laughed. "Absolutely not, for we both know there is a higher position awaiting you when you take your uncle's place as Bishop of Paris."

Henri lifted his chin toward Antoine, bowed again to the king, and walked away.

"Now to Saint-Germain!" the king cried, steadying his hawk and turning his horse around.

"Be alert," the guard warned Antoine as he wheeled his own mount in a tight circle. "It is five leagues to the chateau, but you can watch me eat my saddle if we do not get there in less than half an hour."

2

ROYAL
FRIENDSHIPS

As soon as the company of riders reached Saint-Germain the king dismounted with the white hawk on his hand. A thin nervous man came from the stables to greet him.

"That's Luynes, the king's chief falconer," the guard whispered across the silver braiding on his shoulder to Antoine. "See him wincing? Something's wrong."

"You are late, Sire." The falconer took the hawk onto his own gloved fist. "There are nobles waiting for you on the side lawn. They have arranged a luncheon." The man frowned as he spied the mud on the gyrfalcon's feathers.

Without a word about his troubles at Villepreux, the king turned to check his horse's bridle. "I come to Saint-Germain to be alone. Turn those men away."

"But they are courtiers," the falconer said. "It is their privilege and duty to provide company for you. An hour at their table will not ruin your day."

"My time is already planned," the king huffed, suddenly looking at Antoine. "I have brought a new page from the de Gondi estate. I promised him a horse."

"Surely you joke." Luynes's eyebrows rose. "You want me to tell noblemen—including Monsieur Girard from Vire—that you won't meet with them *because of a boy?*"

"Ahh, Monsieur Girard is here?" The king raised his hand. "That's a different matter. Tell him straight out: I do not wish to see him at all."

"But he arranged the meal."

"It's no act of generosity, I assure you. Everywhere I go, he is there. His words are sweet as rose water to my face. That's because he wants me to give him the abbey that borders on his land. But behind my back, I know, he calls me the Fool of France."

"Perhaps you should just give him the abbey, Your Highness. That would convince him to like you more."

"I have my day planned," the king replied. "Come, Antoine, I will show you my horses."

The falconer surveyed Antoine with a cool eye as he slid from the lieutenant's horse. As soon as he reached the king, two guards in gold-and-white vests hemmed him in. Antoine looked uncomfortably at the pistols tucked into their belts. Noticing his glances, the king shook his head. "Two white-clad guards form my constant shadow, Antoine. You will get used to it, once you begin at court."

The heady smells of oiled leather and hay filled Antoine's nose when they entered a gray corridor lined with stalls. "These horses are gifts from the Queen of England." The king pointed left and right with his short leather whip. "Perhaps you will like one of them."

Antoine, dazed with excitement, walked on tiptoe. As he passed the first stall, the blond nose of a curious horse reached across the wooden gate to nudge his ear. Antoine laughed at the tickling of hot breath against his cheek.

"She's a fine one," the king said, coming up behind him. "In the field I find her full of spirit without a trace of stubbornness."

Antoine touched the velvet skin around her nostrils. "You're a jonquille, if I ever saw one," he teased quietly. "That yellow face and hair of yours remind me of the flowers that bloom in Provence."

"Jonquille!" The king grinned. "A good name for a mare as neat and smart as she."

Antoine let his hand slip from the horse and went to the next stall. The king, however, did not move on. "I'm surprised," he said. "I thought you'd choose her."

"Oh, Your Majesty, I could not take a horse *you* favor!"

"Nonsense!" The king threw back the bolt on the stall door. "Curry and brush this one," he said to the two silent grooms who stood by the wall. "Put a saddle and bridle on her. We will leave for Paris immediately."

Antoine's fingers were clammy when a stable worker finally slid the reins into his hand. Proudly he led his beautiful horse out into the afternoon sun. The king and his guards were already sitting in their saddles, ready to ride. Antoine mounted quickly, and the king rode up to him. "Our race to Saint-Germain showed me you are at ease with horses. Now if you think you can keep pace with me, I would like to take you to Paris by the route that has hedges and fences—but no gates."

Antoine saw the twinkle in his eye. "I am used to cross-country riding, if that is what you mean," he replied. He glanced at the young man's royal emblem to remind himself that this tanned, energetic horseman was his king.

"Gentlemen, let's show Antoine some of the country-side before heading for the palace," the king called as he kicked his horse.

Squeezing his knees against the saddle, Antoine raced after the king. When the Sovereign of France jumped his mount over a high rail fence, Antoine did not hesitate to follow. As Jonquille cleared the wood cleanly, he saw the king look back with a glance of approval. Thrilled by Jonquille's flawless response to his rein and voice, Antoine leaned into the wind. The sights and smells of the summer countryside rushed by him with the glorious feel of a clear, fast stream.

Hour after hour they must have ridden, since the sun was dropping in the sky. But Antoine had no sense of time. Late in the day, the king led the way to higher ground by going over a low stone wall. Antoine took Jonquille over the barrier easily, but as the mare's feet touched down, he felt her shoulders lurching left. The next thing he knew, he was tumbling over the horse's head. He landed flat on his back in dry, sharp grass.

The king dismounted in an instant. He ran to Antoine and knelt beside him.

"Jonquille!" Antoine cried, making himself sit up.

"She is unharmed." The king nodded to the guard who rode the black horse. He had caught the reins of Antoine's mare. "But how are you?"

Antoine stretched his neck cautiously. "Fine, too. Ahh, Your Majesty, forgive me. I failed by not keeping pace with you—"

The king cut him off. "No, I am the one who failed. I was not looking out for you. This is rough ground. I should have covered it more slowly."

"*I* should have been more careful," Antoine insisted, straightening his knees. "I let myself daydream for a moment. That is why I fell."

"What had you so deep in thought?"

"Oh . . . my brother," Antoine said with embarrassment as he glanced into the king's kind eyes. "I mean no disrespect when I say he looks a great deal like you, Your Majesty. In Romarin we used to do everything together. I was just thinking about some of *our* country rides."

The king pursed his lips. "If he is as close to you as you say, he will be disappointed to learn that you have come to the palace instead of going home to Romarin."

"Oh, no! He would be proud of me for that." Suddenly Antoine's eyes were stinging. "Besides . . . he is not in Romarin. He is . . . at sea."

Antoine felt the king search his face for meaning. "Well, whether he is near or far away, be grateful for him, Antoine," the king said finally. "You may think a sovereign has everything. But I tell you, it is a lonely life. What I would give for the love of a brother such as you have for yours."

Antoine frowned. "I am sorry for you, Sire. If I could . . . I would be your brother or your friend."

The king laughed. "Antoine, your heart is too tender to be a page's heart. As soon as we arrive in the city, you will see what I mean. There, giving is a way of getting. And no one serves, unless he knows he will have a reward for his serving. I am sure that in a little while it will be the same with you."

"Believe me, Sire," Antoine promised, suddenly on his knees. "I will be different. I will serve you—just because you are the king."

Louis the Thirteenth put a hand on his shoulder. "We will see, Antoine, we will see. But even if your heart does change, I will remember the good friendship we did share today." He pushed himself off the ground and dusted his clothes. "I have two saddlebags with food. Let us eat and rest."

When the king went to his horse, the guard who had caught Jonquille crouched beside Antoine. "You say good things to the king. If you keep it up, in a few years any title or office you want can be yours."

"But I meant what I said."

The guard laughed. "Well, keep saying what you are saying now, even if you come to the point of not meaning it anymore. I'm giving you this piece of private advice, because I do not want you to lose the opportunities that come with being the king's favorite."

"Only princes and nobles become favorites," Antoine said uneasily. "Why do you tease me with that word?"

The guard twisted the tip of his black moustache as he stood. "I am not teasing. The king does favor you."

"Come, let's eat," King Louis called to them from where he sat on the grass. "I will enjoy this picnic with a band of good riders more than a thousand feasts."

Just as the king put a slice of bread to his lips, a guard in white struck it from his hand.

"What's the meaning of this!" the king shouted.

"Pardon me, Your Highness," the officer explained. "But food must be checked before you eat it."

The guard who had spoken to Antoine suddenly presented himself to the king with a graceful bow. "Since your regular courtiers and servants are absent, I will taste the food for you. If I die, I trust you will tell Captain Blanc that Mercure Sabre gave his life for his king." The daring man took a pinch of each kind of food.

The others guards watched silently as their comrade chewed. "What do you think, Mercure?" they asked.

The guard suddenly held his breath. Everyone else stopped breathing, too. Then he roared out a laugh. "The food is good!" he said. "Enjoy it. Eat."

The king gave the handsome black-haired guard a tired little smile. "Even though you did not die, Lieutenant, I will commend you to your captain."

Mercure bowed and came to sit with Antoine, who could not help admiring the man's courage.

"You could have been killed," Antoine whispered.

Mercure shrugged. "I am a good gambler! As such I reap more than my share of rewards. Now, help yourself to food."

When everyone had finished eating, the king called out, "Let's ride!"

Instead of going through fields they followed a hard dirt road. The guards in white carefully flanked Louis the Thirteenth now, and Antoine dropped behind them. Mercure rode at his side. "Do you know Paris well?"

"No, not at all," Antoine replied.

"Then I will tell you a little about your new home." The guard grinned. "You see the Seine River on our right. That flows through the city. The first cluster of houses we will pass makes up what is called faubourg Saint-Honoré. I believe your de Gondi friends own prop-

erties there. I would be glad to find out, so that you can
visit them sometime."

Antoine nodded. "You have been most kind to me all
day. Thank you, Monsieur."

"Ahh, you must call me *Mercure* as my friends do,"
the guard said with a laugh. "You see, the captain of my
company gave me the name. I'm *Mercure Sabre, the
quicksilver sword,* that shuns no danger."

"From what I've seen already, it's true!" Antoine
said. His excitement grew as they rode through the city
gates. Soon Mercure Sabre was pointing out the huge
Tuileries Gardens and the narrow street leading to the
Louvre itself.

Cries of "The king returns! The king returns!"
echoed as they entered a courtyard blushing with the
light of many cloth-covered lanterns. Military officers,
noblemen, guards, and boys in blue uniforms scrambled
to line the king's way as he rode to a standstill in front of
the door.

The activity spun Antoine's head in every direction,
but the king seemed to notice nothing at all. Giving his
horse to a groom, Louis the Thirteenth dismounted and
went inside. When another uniformed stable worker
grabbed Jonquille's bridle, Antoine jumped down, too.
The king motioned him to follow, then strode down a
dim hall and up a dark set of stairs. All but the two
guards in white dropped back before the king led Antoine into the first room of his private living quarters. It
was a large room, furnished with gold draperies, a glowing chandelier, a round table, and a couch.

"There are papers to sign, Your Majesty, and a letter

that needs your immediate approval and seal," an older man said hurriedly from the door to the king's bedroom.

The king sighed. "I will take them into the other room, but first, Chamberlain, I want to speak with you about a position for this boy Antoine de Romarin."

Antoine dipped his head nervously.

The man scratched his graying beard. "I have no positions at present. The best advice I can give is to find a noble family who will take him in. He can begin his studies with a tutor until a place opens for him."

But the king shook his head. "His father is coming tomorrow. I want to be able to say that Antoine is serving in the palace."

The chamberlain tapped his fingers together. "I have no room for him, but if you are willing to let him sleep on this couch tonight, I could send for him at half past five tomorrow morning. The boy who brings your boots at six is in bed with a fever. For tomorrow, at least, Antoine could have his assignment."

"Good," the king said with satisfaction. "Now good night, Antoine. I have much work yet to do."

Antoine bent his knee before the king. "Thank you, Sire, for the horse, the day—for everything you have done." He caught a glimpse of the king's slight smile.

When the ruler and the guards retired, Antoine stood to face the chamberlain. The old man clucked his tongue. "One more boy," he muttered. "I will send a servant with some refreshments and a uniform for you, young de Romarin. But understand this, if you don't behave well for me, I can cross the king himself and see that you are put out on your ear."

3

SWORDS BEFORE DAWN

Antoine looked out over the dark roofs of Paris until a page, slightly older than he, came to deliver his clothes. "Your supper will be brought within the hour," the boy announced before he hurried out the door. Antoine was surprised. After a day with the king and his men, it seemed strange and disappointing to be alone.

The uniform in his hands, however, cheered him. Quickly he tried on the loose shirt, blue vest, and short ballooning pants, a copy of the outfit he had seen on the other boy. The long mirror on the wall reflected his neat appearance. With satisfaction he watched himself complete the change by fastening the ruffled collar around his neck. Then he had nothing to do but study the rooftops again.

Suddenly the thought of his nightmares seized him. After what had happened at Villepreux, should he risk sleeping in the palace at all? Sitting down on the couch, he began to consider ways to keep himself awake. But even to think about standing or pacing all night made him tired. He closed his eyes for just a moment. His head touched the couch. Before he could stop himself, he slipped into a deep and quiet sleep.

Hours of silent darkness slipped by, but then Antoine's heart started to race. Slowly, like hot coals being blown to brightness, Turk Rodomonte's eyes began to blaze in front of him. Worst yet, the hideous pirate had a hold on his hand. The man leaned close, and for the first time Antoine saw his face. A red gaping hole took the place of Turk Rodomonte's nose! Low ugly scars were all that remained of his ears!

Antoine gasped and struggled to pull away from the horror. But the man would not let him go. Then he made Antoine's fingers touch his face. "Fourteen years ago Comte de Romarin took flesh and blood from me!" the pirate seethed. "Now I will pay him back, by forcing his own flesh and blood to come with me."

"I-I don't understand," Antoine stammered.

"Just tell the comte what I said! When he hears you, he will understand. I have a plan to get you back to him. But first, I'll be taking out those big wide eyes—"

Antoine's fingers were like tight vines around the couch cushion when his body jerked from sleep. "Oh, no!" he groaned. "Have I cried out again?"

Who would find him trembling this time—the chamberlain, a guard, the king himself? Clinging to the couch, he took deep breaths. No one came.

Just then five strokes sounded in a distant tower clock. *It's almost dawn!* he sighed gratefully. *I've made it through the night!* In less than half an hour someone would come for him. Then his only worry would be to please the chamberlain and the king.

He relaxed. But when he turned toward the breeze coming in from the open window, his heart leaped into his throat. A man wrapped in a cloak had one leg across the sill! Antoine ducked between the table and couch and held his breath in the darkness. The intruder's hand moved slowly to his scabbard as he crept to the king's bedroom door.

Antoine bolted for the hall. "Guards! Guards!" he screamed. "Someone tries to kill the king!"

Dazed officers threw down their dice and cards to grab pistols and swords. A whirlwind of guards raced to the king's chambers. Others clattered down the stairs. Antoine ran after them and into the courtyard outside. He saw the intruder slip down from a rope on the second-story window. Guards rushed in from all directions, but Mercure was first to draw his sword.

"In the name of the king, surrender!" Mercure shouted.

But the man leaped aside, his cloak falling from his shoulders. His own weapon whipped the air, then locked itself against the bold guard's outstretched blade.

"It's Girard!" someone shouted as the other guard stepped back to give the two men room to fight.

"I've had enough of the childish ruler!" the nobleman with the sword called out. "If I can't stop him, at least I'll take his guards and run them through." Then with an evil grin and a sudden twist of his wrist, he drew a line of blood down Mercure's neck with his sword.

"Help him!" Antoine cried out desperately.

A man behind Antoine put a hand to his shoulder. "Be patient, page. Mercure may give a little blood for his king, but he won't have to give his life."

"To the death now!" Girard said confidently, his sword flashing with reflected light. But Mercure smirked and thrust his blade deeply into the nobleman's chest. He stepped back calmly and the other man crumpled dead at his feet.

"A good morning's work, Mercure!" The guard behind Antoine came forward to shake his hand.

"Ahh, Captain Blanc!" Mercure said with pure delight. "You saw the fight!"

"Of course." The officer pressed his handkerchief against Mercure's throat to stop the trickle of blood. "But did you also know that the king himself watched you from his window?"

"What fortune!" Mercure said as he raised his eyes. When he saw the king looking down into the courtyard, he knelt on one knee. Uncovering his head, he swept the plume of his hat against the pavement. Everyone who watched him, including Antoine, suddenly followed the guard's example. They stayed bowing until the king nodded to them with pleasure, then disappeared from view.

As Mercure stood, Captain Blanc shook his hand again. "I meet with the king at ten today. Surely by then he will know what reward he wants to put into your hand."

"Hah-hah!" Mercure said merrily. "I think I will hide myself away at the *Merle et Mouton* until you have heard good news." His eyes grew brighter. "In fact why

don't you and all those who were on the nightwatch come with me? We're all off duty now. As a celebration, I will pay for everyone's food and drink."

Antoine could see Captain Blanc considering the idea even as other guards started linking arms around him and Mercure. "Indeed, this is a rare moment of generosity for Mercure Sabre," one man said lightly to the captain. "Surely you won't make us turn down his offer."

The captain shook his head good-naturedly and joined the group. Then looking over his shoulder, he called Mercure's attention to Antoine. "We'll go at your expense, Mercure, only if you are willing to treat the page, too."

"The page?" Mercure said with a lift on his brows.

"You know, the one who sounded the alarm," Captain Blanc said impatiently. "You would not have killed Girard if it had not been for this boy with strong lungs."

Mercure's gaze met Antoine's. "Why, I know him. That's Antoine de Romarin. You were the one who screamed?"

Antoine nodded.

"Well, Page de Romarin, welcome to our group."

Antoine hesitated as the rowdy band of men made their way toward the courtyard gate.

"Come along, Antoine." Captain Blanc looked back. "Mercure will buy you breakfast, but don't be late."

Before they could leave, however, another officer in a different style of uniform pressed through Captain Blanc's company. In his right arm, he pulled a beardless peasant man who had his hands tied behind his back.

"Who is the prisoner?" Mercure asked, bristling for more action. "Does he know the dead Girard?"

Antoine saw the captive flinch at Mercure's words. Still, the man looked straight ahead, hiding well any feelings he had of fear or sorrow.

"He was found with the nobleman's horse outside the gate," the officer reported. "Apparently he was told to stand by the mount until Girard returned."

"And what is his name?" Mercure asked.

"He won't tell me anything else, Monsieur."

"My goodness, man, when *I* have a prisoner, I can make him say anything I want."

"Watch yourself, Mercure," the captain warned.

"I wouldn't hurt him." Mercure Sabre laughed. "But look! The king is watching from the window again. Allow me to present the prisoner to His Majesty. We will let Louis the Just decide what should be done with him."

Antoine jumped aside as Mercure roughly pushed the prisoner forward. He made him stand beside Girard's body as the king looked down. "Sire, I present the servant to the man who tried to murder you. What shall be done with him?"

The king put his elbows on the windowsill. "That cannot be Monsieur Girard's attendant. His servant would be dressed in silks, not rags."

"Then tell the king who you are!" Mercure demanded as his dark eyes flashed toward the somber man.

The red-haired peasant said nothing.

Mercure drew his sword. "I will cut you down if you do not show respect. Now tell the king who you are."

The man dropped to his knees and made an awkward bow. "I am a laborer on Monsieur Girard's estate," he said steadily. "I owed a debt I could not pay. Monsieur assured me it would be forgiven if I came with him to Paris and obeyed him without fail."

"There you have it," Mercure said to the king. "This man assisted Girard in his plot. You have heard his confession. What shall his punishment be?"

The king stepped back from the window. "Take him to the Bastille," he said wearily. "If the jailer finds him sound of body and mind, have him sentenced to three years in chains behind a galley oar."

The peasant fell to the flagstones as though the king had robbed him of his bones. His lips stayed silent, but he looked at the guards and at Antoine with angry eyes.

"Get up, you bag of rags," Mercure ordered. "The officer of the gate will take you to the prison." The guards chuckled as Mercure's swordtip pricked him in the pants to make him rise.

When the man had been led away, Captain Blanc and Mercure put Antoine between them. They joined the singing, laughing band of men that finally paused under the painted sign of a crow and a sheep—the *merle* and *mouton*.

Inside the windowless tavern, Mercure pressed his purse against an old woman's grease-stained apron. "Here's three times what your cooking's worth, Mam'selle. Now I want breakfast for all of us—and drinks."

Captain Blanc sat down beside Antoine on one of the

benches at the table. "You are new at court, no? That means you may not yet understand my company's behavior when we are at rest. These men work hard. So, when there is a reason to celebrate, I let them play hard, too."

Mercure's riding spurs scratched another bench as he sat across from them with his legs stretched out on the seat. "So, my captain, tell me. Was my swordfight today worth a promotion to the company of the king's most-trusted bodyguards?"

The captain chuckled. "Mercure, only the king can decide that. You must wait until ten. Remember? That is why you're here."

"Yes, you're right. So I will make the most of my time." Suddenly Mercure was standing on the table. "Listen, my friends. Today I will receive a king's reward. Now if any man cares to give the captain here his private guess as to the exact amount of this prize, I will consider it a firm bet. The one who names the precise figure will receive a fifth of the reward."

"Mercure, your head's getting so fat the cook will want to larder her eggs with it." A young guard laughed and raised a tankard of cider.

But most of the others frowned on his salute. "Be careful," they warned, "or he'll change his mind about the gamble."

Captain Blanc looked from Mercure to Antoine as the guard sat down. "That's fine for the company," he said, "but what do you plan to do for the boy? So far, he has only a peasant's hat to show for his loyalty."

"I think he needs a sword!" a third man at their table

said. "I never saw a king's page who did not carry one."

"In your haste you left yours in the palace?" Captain Blanc asked Antoine.

"No, Monsieur," Antoine replied softly. "My father has never let me wear one."

"And why not, may I ask?" the captain said.

"Because he believes a son should earn the right to have a sword. He says a weapon carried by one unprepared to use it properly can do great damage and little good."

"Hah! You have a wise father," Captain Blanc said with a nod. "I will remember to tell him that, if and when we meet." His lips pressed together. "Certainly after your show of courage today, your father will want you to carry one. In preparation for this good event, what would you say to a lesson from the swordmaster who trained Mercure?"

"Oh, yes!" Antoine answered. "But who is that?"

"'Tis I!" the captain said. "Now get on your feet, and I will put you on your guard."

Antoine quickly finished the food on his plate, while Captain Blanc reached behind him to grab a smoking stick from the fireplace. He drew a long, black line of charcoal across the brick floor.

"Place your right toe against the line, like this. And your left heel touches the same line, back there," the captain explained as Antoine stood. His arms flung out in all directions when he tried to copy Captain Blanc's relaxed moves.

"You're getting better." The man smiled. "Now put your left hand lightly behind your back. Hold out your right. There's no need for a sword until you know how to use your fingers, wrists, and feet. Try to follow me."

Antoine had no idea how long the lesson lasted. His arms and legs soon ached, but the captain kept going so he would not admit his tiredness. Back and forth, arm out, arm in, Antoine tried to mirror his instructor. Only when the tavern door swung open did he let his exhausted shoulders rest.

"Father!" Antoine exclaimed as the general and the comte walked into the smoky room. "What are you doing here?"

"I might ask the same of you," his father huffed. "I came to the palace to meet the king. Instead I was met by his chamberlain, who told me you had been irresponsible enough to disappear without a warning."

Antoine's hands went to his face. "Ah, with all the excitement I forgot about the king's boots!"

"The chamberlain is going to throw you out," his father warned, "unless the general and I find some way to mend the situation. We have only until eleven o'clock. Because of the intruder's death, our meeting has been put off until then."

Antoine surveyed their unhappy faces, while Captain Blanc joined them. "General de Gondi," the man said with a nod, "I could not help overhearing the conversation. Your meeting with His Majesty comes just one hour after mine. By then, I will see to it that Louis the Just and his chamberlain know the truth—it was Antoine's quick work that saved the king. Take courage, Monsieur de Romarin. By this evening, your son will be back in the palace court."

4

THREATS FROM A FOOL

The carriage rocked through the streets as Antoine and his father rode with the general to his city house. When the short trip ended, Antoine pulled back the leather window flap for a first look at the brick mansion, with its private stables and gardens. A coachman opened the carriage door, and they followed General de Gondi up the walk. "The women should be home from their visit to the palace," he said. Even as he spoke, Madame de Gondi and Antoine's mother came out from the house.

"Antoine, you're here!" She quickened her step. "I was so worried when I heard the chamberlain couldn't find you!"

"Antoine saved the king!" Comte de Romarin boasted carelessly.

His mother squeezed Antoine. "Oh, I hope you didn't see the swordfight we heard about."

"But I did." Antoine pulled away. "Mercure Sabre the guard fought well. And afterward, I got a saber lesson from the company's captain, who taught Mercure himself."

His mother sighed fearfully, but his father grinned. "Antoine! The courage you have gained since being in the king's service! You hardly seem like the same boy we brought to Villepreux."

"Then, Antoine, you saw Monsieur Girard himself?" Madame de Gondi said excitedly.

"Yes, Madame, when he climbed into the palace window."

"And his servant? Your mother and I heard that this man was taken to the Bastille. Did you see him, too?"

"Y-Yes, Madame." Antoine winced. "His angry eyes will not be easily forgotten."

"Then God be praised!" the woman exclaimed. "Antoine de Romarin, you are the answer to my prayers!"

Antoine's mother twisted her handkerchief nervously. "What are you thinking, my friend?"

"Corinne, don't you see?" Madame de Gondi's eyes were glowing. "We can send Antoine with Monsieur Vincent. Antoine can point out the right prisoner to our priest. Then Monsieur can ask the man himself who the girl is and what should be done with her."

"What girl?" Antoine asked.

Madame de Gondi's pale complexion grew pink with excitement. "Right after the swordfight, one of the queen's attendants found a peasant girl about your age hiding in the courtyard gardens. Your mother and I saw her ourselves. She ate some bread and honey, but she will speak to no one. You see, then, to find out who she is, Monsieur Vincent must talk with the prisoner."

"Antoine does not have to be involved," the comte said to General de Gondi. "In Romarin we let the poor take care of themselves."

"You cannot mean this." Madame de Gondi sighed. "Comte, you call yourself a Christian, don't you? If we do not show compassion, God himself may hold us accountable for the sufferings of others."

The comte raised his eyes to the general. "And if God made us help all the poor, soon we would be poor ourselves," he grunted.

The general nodded. "That is probably true. But you should understand my wife's interest in charity. Each week we give our priest time and funds to help the poor on our estates, in the hospitals, and in the prisons."

"Please, Comte," Madame de Gondi begged. "Let Antoine go with our priest."

The comte stroked his beard. "As a gentleman, I am required to assist a lady in distress. For this reason—and this reason alone—I give my permission for Antoine to go."

The next time General de Gondi's coach rattled through the streets, Antoine sat on one of its leather-covered seats with a large soup pot between his knees. Monsieur Vincent, across from him, steadied two baskets filled with bread.

"The Bastille," the coachman announced when the carriage stopped and he opened the door. "Shall we wait, Monsieur? I know it is your habit to walk in Paris."

The priest looked at Antoine as he lifted the bread baskets from the coach. "Yes, please do wait."

Antoine lugged the heavy kettle into the shadow of the prison. Outside the closed doors, Monsieur Vincent paused to speak. "It is not going to be pleasant in there." These words would have frightened Antoine more if the man's eyes had not been bright and his voice kind. "Before we go in, I want to know if you understand the reason for Christ's death."

The question startled Antoine. He answered in the best way he could, by reciting a few Latin words from the creed of faith his mother had taught him years ago. *"Qui propter nos homines et propter nostram salutem. . . .* For us men and for our salvation he came down from heaven. He was crucified for us."

The priest's forehead wrinkled. "You have had good instruction, Antoine. God help you understand what you have just said. You will hate the men you see in here—unless you see Christ himself in their distress. Let their disgrace remind you that our innocent Lord Jesus suffered as a prisoner, too, just so we could be freed from sin."

Antoine was silent. Never before had he heard a priest talk about God without an altar and a prayer book. The man closed his eyes for a moment. Then the huge latch creaked in his hand. Right inside the door, they came face-to-face with a guard. "So you're back, Holy Man," the jailer said looking at the food. "Go inside, but know this, Vincent de Paul, I would keep you out if I could." His iron key clicked into the lock of a huge black gate. "It was much quieter in here before you started coming. Then we just stripped the meanest of men and let them starve."

Monsieur Vincent blinked painfully. "But Christ loves all men, Jailer. He wants every man won over to him."

The man swore. "Preach to your animals, not to me."

Antoine shivered as the gate swung open and then locked behind them. The smells of urine and sweat clawed at his nostrils. He shuffled down the dark hall behind the priest, finding it almost impossible to breathe.

"Monsieur Vincent. . . . Father Vincent. . . ." The damp stone walls began to echo the cries. Chains clinked, and for the first time Antoine noticed that they were surrounded by the thin dark forms of men. The stench of the matted straw they lay on was stirred up as they struggled to their feet. "Father," called a man on the left. "Feed this one first. It has been two days since he had food."

Without hesitation, the priest waded in to hand out chunks of bread. "Antoine," he called back over his shoulder. "I will hand you a cup. Fill it, and give it back to each man as we move along. There will not be enough soup to go around today, but we will feed the ones who depend entirely on Madame de Gondi for their food."

Antoine took each grimy cup with his fingertips. He dipped one after another into the kettle and then handed them back, avoiding the thin gray hands that reached out to him. The prisoners were like animals, the way they slurped and cleaned their cups with their tongues. But here and there Antoine heard a muttered prayer. And more than one hollow-eyed man drew the invisible sign of the cross against his forehead and chest before he ate.

"Father, . . . please—," a weak voice called from one of the many narrow indentations built into the wall. "Tell me if there is any news about the house in Saint-

47

Roch." The man who spoke had black swollen feet that kept him flat on his back in the filthy straw.

"Oh, Simon," the priest said, kneeling beside him. "I have a meeting about it with the king and the general of the galleys tonight. It is a very good time to pray."

"I do pray." His brief smile showed his lack of teeth.

"I know." Monsieur Vincent gently rubbed some color into his hands which lay against his chest.

"If I do not live to see you get that house for prisoners, I will still rejoice. Another sick man can take my place once it is yours."

The priest lightly brushed his forehead. "Your fever has returned. I will come tomorrow morning, Simon, to hear your confession and to pray with you. It is possible you *will* go to Paradise before I have a house for prisoners."

"Don't worry," Simon whispered. "I have enough strength to say my prayers until tomorrow."

Antoine turned away, embarrassed by the prisoner's sudden tears. As he did, he saw the reason for his being here. "Monsieur Vincent?" he whispered nervously. "I see the man you want. He's the red-haired one with the big shoulders who stands chained to the wall."

Monsieur Vincent took a piece of bread and approached the prisoner. Before he could speak, however, the peasant spit at him. "Don't come near me," he warned. His bare arm muscles strained as he pulled on the rings that pinned his wrists.

"I am a priest, sir. It is my desire to help."

"The only one you'd want to help would be the king," he raged. "You brought a palace page who could recog-

nize me. That is proof enough that you will do me harm."

"No, we came because of a girl who may be—"

"Shut your mouth!" The man kicked straw up toward Monsieur Vincent's face. "Get out of here! If I could, I would do what I did to the guards this morning—try to break your necks."

"The man is a fool! No wonder he is chained like that," Antoine whispered as the priest stepped back to him.

"I don't think so," Monsieur Vincent responded. "Rage often is a cover for hurt or fear. Dip some soup for me. I'm going to try again to talk with him."

Monsieur Vincent approached the prisoner cautiously with the cup in his hand. "The guards have stripped you to your waist, sir. Because I come here almost every day, I know this means no one is paying the jailer to feed you or bring you clothes."

The man against the wall eyed him like a nervous lion.

"You must be hungry. I will help you eat." Monsieur Vincent almost had the soup to the man's lips, when three prisoners who were watching started to call out threats. "Don't tempt the bull with food, Priest. He knows you work for the king. Then next thing we know he will be hanging there dead from the poison in your cup."

"There is no poison—," Monsieur Vincent said.

But the peasant was already wild. With a violent toss of his head, he knocked the soup from the priest's hand.

"Ah, bull, steady yourself," one of the prisoners shouted. "We can do better than spill broth on him."

"Yes, if we don't want a visitor in prison, we have a way to make him leave," another growled.

"Watch out, Monsieur!" Antoine screamed as the man closest to the wall hurled a pail of toilet water in his direction. The priest ducked instantly as the putrid liquid splashed beyond his head and slapped against the prisoner chained to the wall. The trapped man gagged and vomited while days-old urine dripped from his head and face. Antoine turned his back on the awful scene to see two guards with bullwhips racing past him.

The air crackled from a long tongue of leather that landed inches from the three prisoners' feet. "Get to the wall, you dogs," the jailer with the keys ordered before snapping his whip again.

Monsieur Vincent grabbed the jailer's wrist. "Stop this! Please! Don't hurt them. Look at me. There is no harm done."

The jailer turned to the priest with the weapon in his hand. "I long to use this on you, troublemaker! I told you before. We would not have any problems if you would let a few of these beasts die."

Monsieur Vincent looked silently at each panting, wide-eyed prisoner who watched him. "I would like some water—and some soap," he said finally.

"You think this is an inn!" The jailer yelled in a fury. "Go home to Madame de Gondi smelling like a barnyard. Then maybe she will stop sending you here."

But the older guard left them for a few minutes. He returned with a pitcher and a rag. "This is the best I can do, Monsieur," he said, "At least wash your hands."

"Thank you." The priest waited until the guards

walked away. Then, instead of washing the stench from
his own body, he approached the silent, withdrawn peasant who now hung on his chains. Monsieur Vincent
poured some clean water on the man's red hair.

"Oh, Monsieur. . . ." The prisoner sighed. Then he
went on with other soft, sad words that Antoine could
not quite hear while the priest slowly wiped his face and
neck and back.

Monsieur Vincent, with the skill of a stable worker,
kicked away the soiled bedding from the prisoner's feet.
He found a wooden pitchfork along the wall and tossed
in three clumps of cleaner straw. Antoine saw the man
and the priest exchange one last silent glance as Monsieur Vincent put the pitchfork away. "Get the kettle,"
the priest said to Antoine. "Our work is finished here."

Antoine's skin tingled with relief when they finally got
outside. Monsieur Vincent followed him into the coach.
"Ahh, God be praised," the priest said, sitting rigidly to
keep the back of his stinking robe from touching the
seat. "One vile bucket was enough to win a man's trust."

"He was speaking to you as you washed him?"

"Yes. His name is Thomas Martel. And because he
warned his daughter to trust no one if they were sepa-
rated in Paris, he is sick with worry for her. As soon as I
change out of these clothes and talk with Madame
de Gondi, I must visit the child at the palace. She needs
our help."

5

STOLEN PROPERTY

In his parents' room at the de Gondis' house, Antoine found a flask of sandalwood oil. He rubbed the spicy liquid on his hands and face to chase away the odors of the Bastille. Then wearily, he sank down into a chair. Hours later his mother found him napping there.

"Your father has returned from the palace with great news!" she said as Antoine stretched his arms. "The king is going to release *two hundred* prisoners to be oarsmen on our galleys—just because of your bravery today!" She laced her fingers. "You must come outside to the rose garden. The de Gondis are providing an afternoon repast of fruit and pastries as a celebration for us."

As soon as Antoine was seated at the table between his parents, his father burst forth, "The king could not stop praising you, Antoine!"

Across from them General de Gondi nodded in agreement. "It is true. In five weeks some older pages will be transferred to other positions, and the king wants you back in the palace as soon as that happens. I have offered to have you stay here until then. The king himself has already arranged for your fencing and riding tutor to live with us."

"And I've already put your horse into the general's stable," his father added. "Your teacher should move in tonight. He is the man who killed Girard."

"Mercure!" Antoine exclaimed. "But his captain needs him."

"The man has been given time off for the assignment," his father explained. "Then in five weeks he will return to the palace as one of the king's two closest bodyguards."

The excitement of the sudden changes made Antoine disinterested in the food on his plate. He was forcing himself to taste the cheese when hoofbeats sounded in the driveway beyond the garden. Everyone looked up to see Monsieur Vincent ride in on a white horse. The priest tied his horse near the mansion. He hurried up the garden pathway to their table. Antoine noticed that the dark cassock Monsieur Vincent wore was just like the one that had been ruined in prison.

"The queen's attendants have bad news, Madame," the priest said to the general's wife. "Thomas Martel's girl Gabrielle has run away and no one can find her."

Madame de Gondi grew pale. "Oh, Monsieur, what are we going to do?"

"Nothing!" her husband said. "You tried to help, but you can do nothing for a child who runs away." The general held an empty plate out to the priest. "Father, join us. We would enjoy your company."

"And I yours, General. But I am on my way to

Clichy." He paused, noticing the tears on Madame de Gondi's cheeks. "Madame, you must not worry about the girl," the priest counseled. "Pray for her. Commit her to God. That is the best thing—and the only thing— we can do."

As Monsieur Vincent walked back to his mount, Antoine saw Henri ride into the driveway on *Jonquille*.

"Who gave him permission to ride my horse!" Antoine demanded as he jumped to his feet. He ran down the garden path shouting, "Get down, Henri! That mare is mine!"

Jonquille's teeth were bared as Henri jerked the reins. "The servants tell me you are moving in with us. That means I can ride your horse. If you don't believe me, ask Father." He yanked Jonquille's head around, turning toward the city street.

Too angry to speak, Antoine jumped up and grabbed Henri by the arm. The boy lost his balance, and both of them banged their heads against the cobblestones as they locked arms and tumbled to the ground. When Antoine finally freed a hand, he started punching Henri's face.

"Enough!" It was Monsieur Vincent who pulled Antoine up.

"He stole my horse!" Antoine panted, seeing the disapproving looks of his parents and the de Gondis.

"I only borrowed it!" Henri argued. "Father, I told him to talk with you. Instead, look what he has done." Blood dripped from Henri's hand as he rubbed the bruise darkening across his nose.

"Antoine! You did this!" his mother gasped.

The general looked first at Antoine's father and then at him. "If you cannot promise to be at peace with Henri, I cannot offer you a place in my home."

Antoine shut his eyes against the anger that swirled inside him. "Do you want me to say he can ride my horse?"

"I teach my sons to share," the general answered. "You will follow this rule while you are here."

"I told you so," Henri chanted.

"But he rides so—!" Antoine stopped, trembling as disappointment seeped into his rage. He was not free to cross their wills. If he stayed with them, he would have to please them. And he had no choice but to stay. Without the de Gondis' help he could lose his position in the palace or, worse yet, the king's support for his father's galleys. "All right," he said, staring at the ground. "I apologize. . . . Henri may ride."

"Pardon, General," Monsieur Vincent said quietly, "but I could take Antoine with me to Clichy if you want to give the boys a chance to cool their tempers."

General de Gondi looked at Antoine's silent parents. "Take him. Then we can have some quiet today."

"Well, my son, get your horse," Monsieur Vincent said to Antoine.

Cautiously Antoine passed Henri and pulled the reins from the other boy's hand. As he climbed into his own saddle, he felt Monsieur Vincent's suggestion was a small miracle. It had saved Jonquille from Henri's grasp. Without a word between them, Antoine and the priest rode past the palace, the Tuileries Gardens, and the last city gate.

"Monsieur . . . ?" Antoine finally ventured timidly. "I feel I should thank you. It seems that you may have planned this trip so that Jonquille would be returned to me."

The priest patted his own mare. "Is that what you think?" Laughter hid in his voice. "I am the de Gondis' priest. You are their guest. Perhaps I brought you along to talk about why you almost broke Henri's nose."

Antoine eyed him nervously. "Henri *stole* my horse," he exploded. "I have a right to be mad. He's the most selfish person I have ever seen, yet no one seems to notice it but me." He turned away, too angry to breathe.

The priest stayed silent until Antoine looked at him again. His thin, tight lips were serious. "Antoine, I am not going to tell you how to think, or talk, or act while you live with the general. But I will keep reminding you *whose* you are." He paused. "From our talk outside the prison this morning, I guessed you were a Christian."

"Yes, of course, Monsieur."

"Then you know we can be Christians only because God bought us at a very high price—the blood of his son. God alone has the right to our hearts and minds now. He is more the master over us than you are to that fine horse of yours."

Antoine rubbed the sore spot on the back of his head. "So what does that mean? You want me to give in to Henri every time?"

"No, Antoine. I want you to give in to Christ every time. I will talk with Henri about his actions. But even if he does not change, God can help you to do his will in every situation."

Monsieur Vincent's horse stamped impatiently as he pulled to a stop. "Keep yourself at peace with God, and everything else will come to rest in its proper place."

Antoine sighed. Monsieur Vincent's words were fine for a priest, but if he had the moment back, he knew he would punch Henri again.

"I think that's enough talk for one day." The priest smiled. "I've heard so much about your riding skills, Antoine. Would you like to race to Clichy?"

"Against you?"

"Ahh, you are not afraid to compete against a former peasant who taught himself to ride any creature with a mane and four feet?"

"No!" Antoine adjusted his position in the saddle.

"Good! Clichy will be the next village you come to."

A moment later Antoine tasted the dust kicked up by the priest's horse galloping off ahead. Antoine crouched to ride his fastest, but they had passed the first small homes of Clichy before he caught up with the man.

"You are a good rider, Monsieur!" Antoine exclaimed when the priest finally slowed the pace.

"For a priest, I guess you mean." The man pushed down his small black cap and wiped the perspiration from his eyes.

"For anyone."

Monsieur Vincent chuckled. "God made horses to run, so don't you think we should learn to ride them well?"

Antoine smiled as a breeze cooled his face.

The priest dismounted to lead the way up a thin, curving path to the right. Antoine got down and walked in front of Jonquille to a low stone hut with a thatched roof. "I am the parish priest in Clichy so I bring communion to the ill farmer who lives here," Monsieur Vincent said, taking a book and a small bundle from his saddlebag. "Then I might walk to the next house to speak with the man there about helping his neighbor with his chores."

"May I wait out here?" Antoine asked.

The priest nodded and went to the door.

Antoine took Jonquille and Monsieur Vincent's horse into a lush green pasture. He stretched out on the warm ground, content to watch the clouds while the mares eagerly cropped off mouthfuls of grass nearby. It seemed that he was in Romarin again. He had a sudden longing to show Jonquille to Luc.

A slice of moon was in the sky when the priest was ready to ride home. Antoine saw that the fatigue of the long day hung on Monsieur Vincent's shoulders as they rode in silence. Right outside the city gate, Monsieur Vincent paused.

"Just one more stop today," he said with a tired smile. "The king and the general want to discuss my plan for getting a house near here where sick prisoners can receive decent food and care. I must measure the property and then go to the palace."

"It is the house that Simon prays for?" Antoine asked quietly.

"Why, yes." The priest's eyes brightened. "Not too many boys of your rank would bother to remember a dying convict's name."

Antoine nodded awkwardly, even though Monsieur Vincent's remark made him feel good inside.

"Do you know your way to the de Gondis' from here?"

"Of course."

"God be with you, Antoine. I enjoyed your company today."

Antoine waved to his new friend before urging Jonquille to quicken her pace on the cobblestone street. Inside the city gate candles flickered in some windows and the smell of bacon cooking filled up the spaces among the rows of tall brick houses. When Antoine arrived at the edge of the de Gondis' property, a bright lantern marked the entrance to the carriage driveway. As he passed the corner of the stable built right along the street, he heard low moaning sounds. Between the stable wall and the hedgerow that lined the street, Antoine saw someone lying in the dirt. He dismounted and cautiously pulled back the cloak that hid the man's face.

"Mercure!" he gasped.

The guard seemed to awaken from sleep. "Antoine . . . ? Get me home."

"I'll call the general!" Antoine said.

"No!" Mercure's shout made him clutch his chest. "No. I have a room above the *Merle et Mouton.* . . . Take me there, but don't get anyone!"

6

SECRET
MEETINGS

With Mercure Sabre's direction, Antoine found the *Merle et Mouton* tavern as the injured guard rode behind him. He helped Mercure down. The man leaned heavily against Antoine while he tied Jonquille to a post along the street. "Go in by the back . . . quickly," Mercure whispered. "This would not be a good time to meet any-one."

On the second floor Mercure rattled a key into the lock with shaky fingers. Inside the bedchamber the guard struggled to light a lamp, and the flame tossed gold rings around the cluttered room. Mercure collapsed onto his unmade cot.

"What shall I do?" Antoine's voice was high with worry. "Where are you hurt?"

"Everywhere!" Mercure growled as he reached for an opened wine bottle by his bed. With one hand he unbut-toned his doublet. He splashed some of the alcohol against his chest, and his lips wrinkled in pain.

"Stand back," Mercure groaned. "I am quite capable of taking care of myself."

Antoine caught a glimpse of the new red slash that had joined the scars on Mercure's broad chest. "Is that serious?" he gasped.

"Go sit in the chair," the man ordered.

The guard breathed irregularly as he stared at the ceiling. Finally he turned his head to Antoine. "There's a book on the mantelpiece. Take it down and open it. A gold coin is hidden inside. Take it, in trade for the promise that you will never tell anyone about this night."

Antoine stayed in the chair. "I don't want money," he said. "I want to know that you will be all right."

"Of course, I'll be all right!" Mercure struggled to sit up. "It would be beneath my dignity to be killed by a pack of thieves."

"You must let Monsieur de Gondi know that thieves attacked you right outside his property!"

Mercure gave a sorry laugh. "No, Antoine. I could not—because these thieves all have names I know. They are guards who work at the palace as I do."

"Then the king must punish them!" Antoine cried.

"You young fool!" Mercure mumbled. "As part of your courtly education, I suppose I need to tell you exactly what went on. Four nights ago I played dice with these men. Having some unfortunate luck, I found myself owing a great deal of money that I did not have. Until I killed Girard today, I did not know how I was going to pay these men. But this afternoon, I left the palace with 500 livres in my purse. Since there are few secrets at court, the guards soon knew I had a reward, and they heard that I was to stay as a tutor in the general's house."

"Five hundred livres!" Antoine whistled through his teeth. "That certainly was enough to pay them all."

"You're right. That *would* have been more than enough, if it had not been for the little gamble I made at the *Merle et Mouton* this morning. But six of Captain Blanc's guards guessed that the king would give me exactly 500 livres. And I had made a firm promise that I would give a fifth of the reward to *any* man who guessed the amount."

"So instead of paying one man, you had to pay all six of them?" Antoine did some quick figuring in his head. "Why that means you are *100 livres* more in debt today!"

The guard ran his fingers through his hair. "That is right. I paid off my closest friends first. But as I arrived at the de Gondis' on foot tonight, the unpaid guards drew their swords on me."

"And you held them off?"

"It was three to one," Mercure boasted. "I doubt that anyone is dead, but I bet every man hurts at least as much as I do." His shallow laugh forced him to lie down again.

"What are you going to do, without money or strength?"

Mercure slowly raised his right arm toward the ceiling. "Look, in a day or two I will be fine. The only thing I have to do is to be your tutor. I can manage that." He smiled. "The king is paying me a nice sum for your lessons. Actually, I'm doing fine—if I can trust your silence."

"I will say nothing," Antoine promised.

65

"I will meet you at the general's tomorrow afternoon," Mercure said. He looked around the room suddenly. "I just remembered, I am missing my hat."

"Perhaps I will find it near the de Gondis' gate."

"I would be most grateful if you did," the guard replied. "It has a rare double-diamond clasp that holds the plume in place."

The night seemed eerie as Antoine went back into the street alone. Fortunately Jonquille would get him home fast. But when he got to the hitching post, Jonquille was gone! A barefoot girl stood where his horse had been, holding a dark felt hat in her hand.

"The friend you helped onto your horse lost this in the street," she said quietly. "I followed you here."

Antoine took the hat. "If you have been waiting for me all this time, you must have seen the person who took my horse!"

She nodded. "I know where your horse is."

"Well, where?" Antoine demanded.

"I won't tell you until you help me." She pushed back her straggly red-blond hair.

"What!" Antoine exclaimed. "You are crazy!"

"I need food," she said calmly. "Bring some to me at dawn tomorrow. I will be waiting at the watchtower that stands along the river near the palace gardens."

"And if I do not come, you will keep my horse?"

The girl nodded.

He grabbed her thin arm. "Look here, you louse. You can't make me do anything I don't want to do."

"Hurting me won't get your mare back," she said wincing. "Let me go. Bring me something to eat, and

you will have your horse tomorrow." Her gray eyes were cool with resentment as she pulled away.

"You are the girl who ran away from the palace today, aren't you?" he guessed suddenly, seeing that her eyes were exactly like her father's. "Your father is in prison for helping with a plot to kill the king."

The girl's face paled. She snatched the hat from his hand and ran off down the street. Antoine raced after her, but he soon lost her in the maze of black alleys that zigzagged among the narrow buildings. He walked back to the de Gondis' house in despair.

His father was waiting for him in the chair of his bed-chamber. "Where have you been?" he asked, closing the book in his lap.

Antoine shrugged tensely. "You know. To Clichy with Monsieur Vincent."

His father nodded. "I want to speak with you. You have the best of futures opened to you as long as the king continues to regard you as a favorite. And I gained more than I ever thought was possible by getting so many galley oarsmen." He paused. "But there are two things that could ruin everything—your temper and your dreams."

Antoine gulped.

"Only you can curb your temper."

"Yes, Father."

"Tomorrow the general and several conductors will start putting together two chains of prisoners for the march to the sea. That means I will leave Paris sooner than I expected. Your mother has decided to stay longer, however, to help you through the nights. Starting tomorrow, she will sleep near you to keep you from waking others. Tonight, I will watch over you myself."

"But what will happen next month when I have to go to the palace?" Antoine fretted as he changed his clothes.

His father pulled at his beard. "I don't know. But by then it will be too late for the king to change his mind about his gift of oarsmen. If you lose your place in court, you will just have to come home." His father raised his eyebrows. "I cannot predict how the king will look upon your problem. I have heard that Louis the Just himself is sometimes terrified by dreams. Now go to bed."

"I am not a baby," Antoine climbed the two steps to his high bed. But even as he complained, he was comforted by his father's presence and the light that burned on the candlestand. Soon he drifted into sleep. All night long the *Hirondelle* sailed in and out of his dreams, but before the terrible scene could unfold, the pink light of morning entered the bedroom.

A pang of guilt pricked his heart as he realized his sound sleep came at the expense of his father who still dozed uncomfortably in the chair. Antoine dressed and combed his hair quickly, careful not to wake the man. Remembering how he and Luc used to beg for fresh bread from the de Gondis' cook on their first trips to Villepreux, Antoine decided to try it again in Paris. He followed the fragrance to the big hot oven near the back of the house.

"Antoine de Romarin, I thought you had mended your ways," the old cook teased as he stepped into her kitchen. "But I see you remember that the first boy up in this household always gets two warm slices of bread."

"Yes, I remember," Antoine said politely as he watched her spread each slice with butter. "Thank you, and if you don't mind I will take them to the garden."

Outside, he headed toward the palace garden and the Seine River by way of the shadows along the house. There was no mistaking the watchtower that overlooked the barges already traveling up and down the still, brown water. He stood for a while in its shade. Not seeing the girl anywhere, he finally sat down on the low wall that divided the riverbank from the street.

Almost at once, she came out of the tall weeds behind him and sat down silently at his side.

"Here." He tossed the bread into her hands. "Now I want my horse."

She ate like a stray dog. "Tomorrow, you must bring me food again," she said.

"You promised I would get my horse!" he raged.

The girl caught his sleeve and led him down the steep bank to the river. There, hidden by a cluster of brushy trees, Jonquille stood swishing flies with her tail. Rushing to the horse, he backed her out of the bushes. The girl grabbed Jonquille's bridle as he mounted. "I was hiding in a stable near the road when I heard the fight out in the street last night. I saw enough to know that the hat I have belongs to your friend." She looked up with her cold eyes. "If you do not bring me food each morning, I will take the hat and diamond clasp to the ladies at court as proof that I saw your friend fight with other guards."

"Look, you don't have to bribe me with threats," Antoine said disgustedly. "You can go back to the palace right now. The women will be happy to take you in. I know Madame de Gondi, one of the ladies who spoke to you. She worries about you. Give me the hat, and I will take you to her house."

"No!" The girl's face was tight with fear. "Those women will send me to an orphanage or have me locked inside a convent so that I have to grow up to be a nun."

"Madame de Gondi would not do that!"

"I don't trust anyone—but my father."

"Your father can't help you," Antoine reminded her bluntly. "In a few days I wouldn't be surprised if he's marched off to Marseille."

"Where's Marseille?" the girl asked with sudden panic.

Antoine shrugged. "Along the Mediterranean Coast. Probably more than two hundred leagues south. That's a month's walk!"

The girl still held her head high, but her eyes began to sparkle with tears. "I must see him . . . before he goes."

"Come to the de Gondis' with me," Antoine said firmly. "A priest there named Vincent de Paul has been to see your father. He can help you."

The girl chewed her lip as she searched his face.

"You can trust me," Antoine said. "The people I speak of will do you no harm." Suddenly he looked up to see Henri de Gondi riding his pony along the riverbank.

"What are you looking at?" she asked even more nervous than he.

"I see someone I know. I must go."

"But you just said you would take me if I wanted—"

"Not now!" Antoine turned Jonquille sharply.

"Why are you leaving?" the girl cried at his horse's heels.

"Get away!" Antoine shouted back, but it was too late. Henri's sharp eye had spied them. He grew hot with the embarrassment at being seen with a peasant. And he knew Henri's questions might open the door to Mercure's secret quarrel.

"Who's the girl?" Henri trotted his pony down the bank to him.

"What girl?" Antoine said. Looking back he was relieved to see that she had hidden herself in the brush.

"You know!" Henri said smartly.

"I came down to look at the barges," Antoine lied. "You probably saw a fisherman's child playing in the weeds."

"I saw you talking to a red-haired peasant girl. You're such a stupid country boy, Antoine. Noblemen's sons don't make friends with peasants."

"Friends?" Antoine raged. "Do you think I'd come here to find friends? I'd go to a pig's sty first. You insult me again, and I will break your nose."

"And I will see that Father sends you home to Romarin!" Henri answered just as hotly.

"Because I rode along the river?"

"We don't come here. It's a shabby port. It's a nobleman's shame to be seen here. I will have to tell Father where you were, and you will be in trouble again."

"How was I to know this?" Antoine's heart beat fast. He began to worry that Henri would tell on him.

"Of course, the cook's made pastries for breakfast." He grinned. "If you give me your share of the sweets, I won't say anything to Father."

Inside Antoine was boiling. "All right. I agree."

When Henri rode away, Antoine leaned down and pretended to adjust his stirrup. He saw the girl peering out from the grasses. "Don't show that hat to anyone," he hissed as she crouched in her hiding place. "I will come back for you."

"Don't bother!" Her voice trembled. "You'd rather help a pig!"

"I didn't mean that!" Antoine said. "If that boy had not come just now—"

But the girl hid her face in her arms, refusing to listen.

"Are you coming?" Henri called down, already on the other side of the wall.

"Of course," Antoine shouted back. He did not dare to look at the girl again.

When the boys rode in the driveway together a few minutes later, the general and Antoine's father greeted them with smiles. "It is good to see that the sons of friends *can* be friends," Monsieur de Gondi laughed. "Right after breakfast you two must come with us to the Bastille. It is quite a sight to see men readied for a march."

Henri nodded enthusiastically, but by the time he had finished his eggs and his *two* pastries, he found an excuse to stay home. Because of Mercure's injury, however, Antoine decided to go with the men. He might need a reason for not meeting with his tutor early in the day.

It was a fine bright morning to be riding through Paris. All along the way women curtsied and men tipped their hats to greet the two well-dressed noblemen and the young royal page trotting their horses through the streets. Antoine enjoyed himself immensely, until the

Bastille rose in front of them. Then he could not stop the gasp of shock in his chest.

Weary men, some of them little more than breathing skeletons, stood outside the prison. The general looked at Antoine's father with some concern. "It will take good conductors to get this batch to Marseille."

"I am glad you decided to travel with me," the comte said. "I do not want men dying on the way."

The general touched his hat. "We will do our best. The king has already promised the conductors an extra four livres for each live head that arrives at the seaport."

Antoine's father motioned him to dismount near the prison wall. He took him right up to the sour-breathed old turnkey who stood outside the prison door. As each convict was forced out into the sunlight, the turnkey locked an iron collar around his neck. Next Antoine's father led him into the stinking throng so that he could watch blacksmiths pound the neck chains into a common line that ran between the pairs of sullen men.

"May I go now?" Antoine asked, when his father and the general had finally completed their inspection.

"All right," his father said with a note of disappointment. "I suppose Mercure Sabre is waiting."

Antoine hugged Jonquille around her warm, strong chest before he climbed up into the saddle. As he reined away from the Bastille, he saw the turnkey pushing another prisoner out for his collar. It was Thomas Martel!

Something close to fear made Antoine watch the iron band click into place around his neck. Suddenly Antoine wished Monsieur Vincent were here. Then with a shiver, he kicked Jonquille into a fast trot toward home.

7

STORMS OVER PARIS

When Mercure Sabre arrived at the de Gondis' house late that afternoon, Antoine was relieved to see him well. Even though dark clouds piled up in the sky, Antoine's new tutor had him ride through the city while he explained the commands given to mounted pages during processions with the king. After that, they joined the de Gondis and Antoine's parents for dinner. Though the food was excellent, Madame de Gondi kept frowning.

"What is it?" her husband finally asked.

"I am worried about the prisoners going to Marseille. It is cold for June. Each man should have been given shoes and a blanket."

"Don't worry, my dear," the general replied. "This afternoon the conductors marched both chains off to the cattle barns south of Paris on the road to Auxerre. They will have protection there. The comte and I will be joining them right after dinner so we can see that everything goes well." When his answer did not cheer her, he spoke again. "What else is on your mind?"

Her small red lips drew together. "Don't be angry

75

with me, but I just can't stop thinking about young Gabrielle Martel. The poor girl has to be hiding somewhere in the city."

The general huffed. "I knew Monsieur Vincent shouldn't have told you her name today. I knew it would make you think about her even more."

Henri kicked Antoine's ankle under the table. "Is she the girl you saw?" he whispered.

"You promised to say nothing," Antoine said between clenched teeth. "I don't want trouble with your father."

"Let's see . . . a strawberry tart will keep me silent." Henri grinned.

In anger Antoine pushed his dessert across the table.

"Are you ill?" Antoine's mother asked.

"Just not hungry," he lied. "I wish Father were not leaving tonight."

Comte de Romarin smiled. "I met with Captain Blanc today, and I have a great gift for you before I go away." He stood, pressing his fingers against the tablecloth. "Come, I will make the presentation now."

As soon as Antoine stood beside him, the man unbuckled the scabbard that held his sword. Silently he fastened it around Antoine's waist. "This is a token of my faith in you," he said. "And it is the best way I know to say good-bye."

Antoine gripped the hilt of his father's sword, unable to speak.

"That looks fine on you, Antoine de Romarin," Mercure said, breaking the room's silence. "When your father returns to Paris next year he will be proud to see that you have learned to use it well."

General de Gondi pushed himself from the table. "I hate to say it, Joseph, but we must be on our way in less than an hour. Before we begin, however, I want all of you to attend vespers with us." From Mercure Sabre to Petit Jean, everyone dutifully followed the general into a small candlelit room on the first floor of the house. The doorman, the cook, and some of the stablehands were already there, kneeling in the last of the three rows of plain wooden chairs.

Antoine dipped a knee toward the altar when he came into the room. Then he slipped into the only available seat, the one beside Henri in the second row. Antoine's sword clunked against the chair legs as he knelt for the opening, silent prayer. Henri snickered. Antoine closed his eyes for a moment to ignore him.

General de Gondi walked to the altar. He bowed to Monsieur Vincent before reading from the book in his hand. "*Jube, domne, benedicere*: Pray, Father, a blessing."

Monsieur Vincent, wearing a white robe over his dark cassock, faced them with uplifted arms as he pronounced the blessing: *Noctem quietam et finem perfectum.* . . . A quiet night and perfect end be given to us by God Almighty."

"Amen." Antoine stood with the others. His sword banged the chair again. Henri made a face at him as his own scabbard moved silently in the row. Hot with embarrassment, Antoine pressed the weapon to his leg. He did not take another easy breath for the next half hour.

When the anxiety of managing a sword in church had ended, Antoine hurried to the stairs to be alone. Mercure, however, came after him. "We must talk about your lesson times for tomorrow."

Antoine stopped on the third step up, unnerved by the guard's pale face. Mercure took a quick, sharp breath.

"Your wound still hurts," Antoine guessed.

"So what if it does? A nobleman knows how to keep his pain to himself!"

They stopped talking as Henri and Petit Jean started up the stairs. Because they would not speak in front of him, Henri pushed his scabbard against Antoine's as he passed. Twisting his moustache, Mercure smiled when Henri stopped at the upstairs railing to try listening again. "Antoine, let's show your sword to the king tomorrow," he proclaimed loudly.

Antoine saw Henri's face before he stomped off above their heads. "I know you said that just to anger Henri," Antoine said. "But the truth is, I wish I could see the king again."

"Then you will—tomorrow morning!" Mercure answered. "First, however, I must get a hat. No nobleman goes to court without one."

Antoine froze, fearing Mercure might press him about the missing hat.

"I will take you to the Halles before we go to the palace tomorrow. You may watch me purchase one there." The guard climbed the stairs with Antoine and stopped at the first bedchamber door. "It's a shame to have to buy another. With my limited funds, I will not get something as grand as the hat and clasp I had before."

Antoine nodded sympathetically as he let himself into his own room. He sat down on his bed and stared at his sword for a long time. Why was he not happy with his father's gift? Finally he changed his clothes. There was a gentle tap at his door. He climbed into bed and called for the visitor to enter. It was his mother. With all the events of the evening, he had forgotten to dread the night. As she entered and sat beside him, his fears returned.

"I am here so that you do not cry in your sleep," she said.

"I know." Antoine turned his head in shame. He blew out the candle and slid from the covers. "At least take the bed. I will spend the night on the chair."

In the darkness she found his hand. "Wait—Antoine. Do you think it would be foolish to pray for peace for you?"

He was silent with surprise. Though his mother had taught him his catechism and had watched him take his first communion, he had never heard her say a prayer outside a church. "I don't know. What makes you want to?" he asked.

He heard her sigh. "Madame de Gondi is so certain that God hears us and cares about us. Being Christian is not just a religion to her, but a relationship with God. Tonight when we sang Saint Ambrose's hymn, I thought . . . if God really does hear prayers like that, he can give peace to you." She squeezed his fingers harder. "Would you pray with me now?"

Awkwardly he knelt beside her as she began the familiar childhood prayer.

"Lord of constant mercy, keep
watch around us while we sleep.

Evil dreams put Thou to flight,
with all phantoms of the night;
Save us from the things we dread,
as we slumber in our beds.
Father, what we ask be done,
through Thine ever-blessed Son,
with the Holy Ghost and Thee,
reigning God eternally. Amen."

The room was quiet for a long time, "Antoine. . . . I believe God was listening. . . . Do you . . . ?"

"I don't know. I guess we'll see tonight." He felt his way to the chair. The wind rattled the window above him as he sat down. Black drops of rain flowed down the glass. He fell asleep thinking of Gabrielle Martel hiding someplace in the rain, and wishing he had not turned her away.

It seemed to be only moments later when Antoine awoke, stiff and chilly in the chair. The first thing he thought was that he had not dreamed! The second thing he noticed was that it was late. His mother was already gone. A loud knock throbbed against the door. He jumped to answer it. Mercure stood in the hall. "For a boy going to see the king, you don't seem too excited about getting up. Put on the king's uniform. Don't forget to wash your face and comb your hair. And hurry. The best hatter's booth in the marketplace opened at dawn."

Antoine, still groggy with sleep, pulled on his clothes. When his hand went for his sword, he paused. He buckled it over his hip, but it still seemed to belong more to his father than to himself. He went into the hallway, only to have Mercure send him back for his cloak. "It might rain again," the guard warned, "and no one visits the king unless he looks his finest."

They went to the market on foot. In the thick crowds, Mercure found the hatter's booth. Antoine saw how much it pleased the guard when three young women gathered to watch him try on hats. "The choice may be more difficult than I thought," Mercure whispered to Antoine. "Here are two coins. You've had no breakfast. Go enjoy some gingerbread while I decide."

Antoine left Mercure grinning into the mirror at his admirers. As he moved up in the line of those waiting for the baker's wares, he came beside a group of dirty children. They leaned on crutches and held out wooden cups. "Coins, please. . . ," they begged. Antoine steadily ignored them, until he saw one pair of cold gray eyes.

"Gabrielle!" he called out.

She pulled back. "How do you know my name?"

"Your father told Monsieur Vincent," he said quickly.

Her lips trembled. "How is my father?"

Antoine heard the distress in her voice. He answered as gently as he could. "He has been moved from the prison."

"Then he *is* being marched to Marseille!" Her head dropped suddenly. She began to sob.

Antoine reached for her. "You have to come with me—"

But a dirty-faced boy beside her hissed, "If old man Crin catches you taking his property, he'll kill you and break both her legs."

Antoine stared at Gabrielle's roughly bandaged knees. "Then you are not really hurt now?" he said with hope.

"Not yet." She closed her eyes. "But soon. Crin cripples all the children he controls, so people pity them more. Then he takes all the money from their cups."

"We must get away now!" Antoine cried.

At the same moment a tense whisper rose from the group. "He is coming."

A husky, bearded man walked up behind Antoine. His breath was hot on Antoine's neck. "So the rich boy has some coins for the poor?" he prodded. "I wish your kind would feed them better. It's a shame the way they're always falling down in the streets and breaking their bones."

Antoine dropped his last coin into Gabrielle's cup as she looked at him in horror. "I give everything I have to this one." His voice shook.

The man roared, "I like to see the children of the rich tremble just as easily as the orphans of the poor." With satisfaction he turned to prod others on the street for their coins.

"I will bring the priest and come at dusk for you," Antoine whispered. "Where will you be?"

"I guess in the pens behind the market butcher shops." Gabrielle shivered. "That's where Crin put me when he found me last night. A sign with two red hens marks the place."

"I promise I will find you." He put his cloak around her shoulders.

"You must take this," she said, pushing something

82

into his hand. "I could not save the hat but give this back to your friend."

"The clasp!" Antoine gasped. "Mercure Sabre will be so glad to get this back, he might rescue you right now!"

Antoine ran back to the hatter's booth. "Mercure, I have your jewel!"

The guard turned. "What fortune! I bought the hat and plume, but I could not make these ladies agree on a clasp." He pinned the jewel into place to hold the new feather.

"It is magnificent!" The young ladies widened their eyes in admiration.

"Quick, Mercure," Antoine pleaded. "Help me save the peasant girl who got it back for you."

Mercure smoothed his hat brim. "I am a king's guard. I don't rescue peasants." He laughed and winked at the women.

"She saved your clasp! You owe her for this."

"*Owe* her, for giving back something that is mine? That is nonsense."

The ladies tucked their curls under their cloaks as it began to rain. "We must get out of this weather before our skirts are marred," one of them said. "Good-bye, Monsieur. We've had a delightful morning."

Mercure turned his back on Antoine until the women waved to him from their carriage window. Then straightening his cloak, he looked at Antoine. "Are you ready for the king?" He stopped. "Where is your cloak? I told you to bring it! No one goes to the palace looking like a wet rat!"

"Go without me!" Antoine shouted as the rain came harder. He turned on his heel, but Mercure caught his cuff.

"You are a king's page, and I have been hired to see that you learn how to handle yourself in court. My success depends on your behavior, so understand that I will give you no choice but to obey me."

Antoine had not seen Mercure like this before. He watched him fearfully.

"Go change your clothes. I will visit the king by myself today, but never let this happen again."

Antoine hurried off through the puddles. When he got home, Henri and Petit Jean were playing cards in front of the fire in the formal sitting room. "Where is Monsieur Vincent?" Antoine panted.

Henri shrugged. "You're supposed to be with the king. What trouble did you get yourself into this tune?"

"I need Monsieur!" Antoine demanded.

"Why?"

"To help me save the peasant girl!" He steadied his quivering chin while Henri laughed.

The boy drummed his fingers on the hearth. "I imagine he is out helping the poor with your mother and mine. We have only eight thousand peasants on our lands. Where do you want to start looking for him?"

Antoine groaned.

"We know they won't be back until late tonight," Petit Jean added. "You can play with us until then."

Antoine ran into the kitchen without answering him. He begged the cook for an extra cloak, saddled Jonquille, and rode back to the market. All day he wandered

among the merchants' stalls, with one eye continually on Crin's small band of roaming beggars. Several times he stopped strangers to ask directions to Auxerre.

Finally, after dark the old man led his hostages to a run-down wooden shed near the sign of the two hens. Antoine kept his distance until Crin locked the door and went away. Then he crept to the shack. "Gabrielle?"

"In here," she cried. "But the door's locked. What will you do?"

Antoine took off his scabbard. With the tip of it, he pried away two loose boards at the bottom of the door.

"I can't believe you came!" she cried as Antoine pulled her out. "What about the other children? Where's your friend the priest?"

"There's no time to talk if you want to see your father!" He pushed her up behind his saddle while some of the beggar children peeked through the broken door. As soon as he mounted, Jonquille galloped down the alley toward the road to Auxerre.

8

CAUGHT IN THE FLOODWATERS

The houses of Paris were far behind them when Jonquille suddenly broke her swift, smooth stride. Instantly Antoine pulled her to a stop. He jumped down and raised her front left, mud-slicked hoof in the darkness.

"What is it?" Gabrielle asked tensely as she dismounted, too.

He let the mare's foot fall. "She's thrown a shoe. Riding her farther could make her lame." Antoine turned his head. "Listen! Another rider is coming down the road."

Gabrielle clutched his cloak. "Could it be Crin?" she moaned.

Before they could move from the road, they were caught in the cloaked rider's lantern light. "Mercure!" Antoine said. "How did you find us here?"

The guard jumped down angrily. "It wasn't easy. But after talking with Henri, I looked for you at the Halles. I've been following you since you freed your peasant friend. I just wanted to see how far you would really go before you realized the folly of your actions."

Antoine felt Gabrielle shiver.

"Get on your horse. You're going back to Paris."

"I can't," Antoine answered firmly. "Jonquille's lost a shoe. Besides, I promised Gabrielle I would take her to her father. He is among the prisoners being held tonight in the cattle barns along this road."

"They're five leagues from here!" the guard grunted. "With a limping horse, you won't get there until close to midnight."

Antoine looked at Gabrielle. "We're still going."

"You show no sense, Antoine!" the guard shouted as they walked on a little way.

"Then why follow us?" Antoine called back.

Mercure rode to his side. "You forget that I am responsible for you. Your father and the general would be furious if I left the two of you out in the night alone."

Rain pelted down as they pressed on in the darkness. They were soaked when, hours later, they arrived at the cattle barns. Antoine was surprised and somehow relieved to see Monsieur Vincent's horse tied near the one building with light streaming from an opened door.

"You go inside and try to explain your actions to your father," Mercure said harshly. "Then I'll come in and make him happy that I at least kept you safe tonight."

Gabrielle squeezed Antoine's fingers. She followed on his heels as he slipped through the doorway. The building was warm from the heat of prisoners sleeping elbow to elbow in thick, clean straw. Alert guards stood watch over the two long rows of men. They eyed Antoine in the candlelight as he searched for the comte. Neither his father nor the general was there, but he found Monsieur Vincent asleep on the floor.

Antoine hesitated, but then bent down to shake the priest. "Monsieur Vincent. I need to speak with you."

The priest sat up immediately. "What is it . . . ? Ahh! Antoine!"

"I never expected to see you here." Antoine felt himself breathing easier.

"Nor I you. I brought supplies that were collected from many Christians in Paris. But why have you come?"

Suddenly Antoine couldn't keep from grinning. "Because I have brought Thomas Martel's daughter!"

The man got up as he spotted Gabrielle standing nervously along the wall. "Come . . . Come, my child," he said excitedly. "I know exactly where you father is."

Monsieur Vincent spoke to the nearest guard as they stopped halfway down the row of still, silent bodies. "Permission for a prisoner to rise," he said.

"Very well, Monsieur. One man may get up."

"Thomas?" Monsieur Vincent stooped to touch the prisoner at his feet. "Wake up. Someone is here to see you."

He did not have to say more. The man, struggling against the weight of his neck chain, rose to his knees and burst into tears. He threw his arms around his daughter. "It's a miracle!" he cried. "I've seen a miracle tonight."

After a long embrace, Gabrielle looked over at Antoine. "A boy brought me here." Her cheeks suddenly colored with embarrassment. "And I don't even know his name."

Thomas reached for Antoine, but his chain stopped

him short. "Bless you, boy." He bit his lip to curb his feelings. "Monsieur Vincent kept telling me to trust God with Gabrielle's life, but until this moment I could not believe that God would listen to a peasant's prayer."

Monsieur Vincent squeezed Antoine's shoulder firmly, but he spoke with concern. "Your father is watching you."

Antoine stiffened. His father stood in the doorway, too tense for words. "Outside—!" he ordered.

Antoine walked into the night with his head down.

"Mercure got me out of my bed in the farmhouse to tell me what's been going on," he said angrily. "You disobeyed him, missed another audience with the king, ran off with a peasant girl, and brought your horse up lame. Anything could have happened to you on the road tonight, if Mercure hadn't been wise enough to keep a watchful eye on you."

Antoine's tongue felt thick with silence.

"Tomorrow Mercure will take you back to Paris. It's a stroke of luck that he has not quit his tutoring assignment in disgust." His father turned on his heel. "Now, stay out of trouble until I call for you in the morning."

Antoine leaned against the wet barn wall and closed his eyes. In a moment Monsieur Vincent came out and stood beside him. The man said nothing, but Antoine felt the comfort of his being there. "You should get some rest," the priest finally said. He took Antoine inside and showed him to an empty space in the straw. He lay down and as the warmth of the shelter soaked into his damp clothes, he found it easy to go to sleep. He did not even think of Turk Rodomonte.

An officer came for him in the morning. He took Antoine to the farmhouse where his father, the general, and the conductors were having breakfast. "It is quite a surprise to see you," General de Gondi said.

"He found the girl your wife has been worried about," his father explained quickly. "He mistakenly thought he should bring her here."

The general smiled. "That was not really a bad idea. My wife is determined to bring us blankets before we start the march. It will please her greatly to see the child."

Antoine ate his eggs in silence while the men reviewed the cost of the trip to Marseille. An officer came to the table. "General, only one ferryboat operator is willing to take convicts across the river in such high water. Do you wish to delay or cross the river now?"

"A day's wait will cost twenty-two livres," one conductor said.

"And a day's delay in getting more protection in the seaport," Antoine's father added.

"Then you are willing to cross?" the general asked.

"We are," the men agreed.

"Have the guards divide the convicts into groups of fifty," the general said to the officer. "Alert us when the first group has been chained together. We will send the men across the water one group at a time."

Antoine's father looked at him. "Get one of the blacksmiths to shoe your horse before they must start moving chains," he said. "I want you back in Paris by noon."

Antoine led Jonquille down to the small lighted forge behind the barn. Because it was drizzling, he stepped inside the back door of the barn to wait while the black-smith finished shoeing his mare. All around him prisoners sat eating black bread in silence. Few seemed even to notice that Gabrielle and Thomas Martel were kneeling in the straw as Monsieur Vincent prayed aloud for them. In the candlelight, Antoine saw Gabrielle's hair glistening with water. Now the priest was baptizing Thomas, too.

Antoine moved into the deep shadows so that he would not be seen. The barn air vibrated with the soft but firm sounds of the priest's low voice. "Thomas Martel, this is the cross of our Lord." With his finger Monsieur Vincent marked the sign of the cross on the prisoner's forehead. "God has redeemed you from sin and death with his own blood." He touched the man's face. "His Holy Spirit has entered into your very being, that God may have your ears to hear his ways—your eyes to see his glory—your nose to smell the sweetness of his salvation—your mouth to speak the words of eternal life." He touched Thomas's chest. "Your shoulders now are for the yoke of his service, and your body will some-day experience the wonder of eternal life with him. Amen."

Thomas stood, stretching his chain as far as it would go. "I have been a servant all my life, Father, to hard and unfair masters. But before I met you, I never heard that God himself desired me for his service. To think the Creator knows me. To think that he would ask me to wait on him with respect and love. Oh, I could not have hoped for anything like this if you had not come to me at the Bastille. Pray that I will serve God well."

Monsieur Vincent wiped his own eyes. "I am certain that you will. Those who love him best serve him best."

"On your feet, every one of you," a guard called from the front doorway. "Stand until you are moved into a group. Any man who talks will get leg irons today."

Monsieur Vincent gave Thomas Martel a silent hug as the prisoner's cheek twitched with emotion. The man leaned down to hold his daughter. Then Monsieur Vincent took her hand and led her outside.

Antoine turned out the back door, his throat swollen shut with feeling. Chains scraped and bare feet shuffled behind him, but he did not look back.

Mercure found him by his horse. No words passed between them. The guard checked the blacksmith's work and then told Antoine to mount. Before they could ride to the road, Madame de Gondi's coach rattled in. She and Antoine's mother stepped out onto the wet ground. Their cloaks were as plain as those worn by farmers' wives.

Antoine saw his father frowning as he came to greet his wife. The general joined them, and when the women put their hands to their faces with wild surprise, Antoine guessed they had been told that he and Gabrielle Martel were in the prisoners' camp. Antoine's mother looked around until she saw him. He rode to her, dismounted, and gave her a kiss.

"You worried me again last night," she said with a teary smile. "But I'm proud of you, Antoine."

Suddenly the air was filled with excitement. Guards swarmed all around them, shouting orders. "The barge has tipped into the water! Get every extra chain! Drive that coach to the riverbank!"

Antoine dropped Jonquille's reins and ran to the river.

"Unhitch those four carriage horses!" The general shouted to his conductors. "Send turnkeys into the water to free as many prisoners as they can reach! We'll pull the rest out with these horses, if we can."

Gabrielle stood beside Antoine, biting her knuckles. Because of Thomas's red hair, Antoine could spot him in the river. He was up to his mouth in water. The men closer to the shore were in little danger. But the men behind him were stranded under the water, the weight of their chains an anchor too heavy to raise.

The screaming prisoners, the frantic turnkeys, and the horses now up to their bellies in water created mass confusion. Of the fifty men who had fallen into the river, Antoine counted no more than forty dripping wet convicts in the heavily guarded group on shore. Thomas was not among them.

"Get the rest of them out!" Antoine's father screamed at the officers and turnkeys who were in the fast, deep water trying to reach the remaining men. They held out the chain that had been connected to the harnesses of the horses near the shore.

"Try again!" the general shouted through cupped hands.

Antoine saw Monsieur Vincent enclose Gabrielle in his arms as she watched the tossed chain explode down into the water once again. Her father disappeared into the murky river. He came up a moment later fighting for breath, the harness chain in his hands.

"He has taken it!" The comte shouted wildly.

The first two carriage horses reached the crest of the bank as the great strong creatures slipped and struggled to pull the tremendous weight of chains and men from the water.

"Come on! Come on!" The guards in charge encouraged them. Antoine could see Thomas's arms stretched by the pull of the heavy chain as his shoulders cleared the water.

Suddenly the wet bank crumbled away. All four horses fell to their knees, sliding back toward the water.

"Father!!!" Gabrielle screamed.

Antoine raced to hold her as Monsieur Vincent jumped toward the sound of Thomas's cries.

"He's being crushed!!!" she groaned.

Antoine forced Gabrielle's face away from the awful scene. He could hear the general shouting for a turnkey to go between the horses. While Antoine held the girl's eyes shut, he watched the men pull Thomas free. The guards succeeded in getting all four horses up the hill and the great burden of men cleared the water behind them. Two guards carried Gabrielle's father over to Madame de Gondi's coach.

"I want to see him!" Gabrielle sobbed.

Antoine trembled. Surely Thomas was dead, but he let her slip away when he saw Monsieur Vincent run to the carriage.

The priest and Madame de Gondi set to work at once bandaging the unconscious man's bleeding arm and shoulder. Antoine watched them through the open door, and Gabrielle stood beside him, pressing tight fists to her chin. When Antoine's mother joined them, Gabrielle buried her face in Madame de Romarin's cloak and wept. Antoine's mother stroked her hair. "My child, whatever happens, we will help you."

The general and the comte looked inside the coach. "All these tears must mean the man has died," Antoine's father said without emotion.

Monsieur Vincent stepped out of the carriage. "No, he lives."

"Then I want to rent a cart from a farmer so that he can be hauled to Marseille," the comte told the general.

"That will kill him!" the priest said.

"We have no choice," the general said, though there was some compassion in his voice. "As long as he lives, he is counted with those going to Marseille. When the rest of the convicts cross the river, he must come, too."

Antoine's mother broke away from Gabrielle. "You should free him! He helped you save the other prisoners. Because of him, not one man died."

"We are under oath to deliver him to the seaport," General de Gondi said to her. "The guards there decide the fate of those too weak to row."

"Let me keep him here until he is well enough to travel," Monsieur Vincent suggested. "You have my word that he will be delivered back to the chain, if he survives."

The general put his lips together. "I might permit that, if the conductors had an officer to spare. We cannot take the responsibility of leaving him unguarded."

"How about Mercure?" Antoine blurted out as the guard approached, leading his own horse and Jonquille.

"I've come to take Antoine back to Paris, now that the excitement seems to be over," the guard spoke directly to Antoine's father.

But the general held up a hand. "Would you take the assignment of guarding the injured man in this coach

until he dies or can be restored to the chain? I will pay
you the wages of a conductor, fifty sous per day."

"You don't want Antoine back in Paris then?" Mercure asked, tipping back his hat.

"Oh, Father, let me stay," Antoine begged.

His mother touched Antoine's back. "I will stay, too,
Joseph, to help Madame and Monsieur Vincent nurse
the man to health."

Comte de Romarin looked inside the coach. "Have
the priest arrange for you to stay in the farmhouse we
used last night, if you wish," he said harshly. "I predict
the man will be dead by morning. Monsieur Vincent can
pay the farmer to bury him, and then you can all go back
to Paris where you belong."

9

PIRATES IN PORT

The colors of sunset swirled across the sky that evening as the women cooked vegetable stew on an outside fire with utensils borrowed from the farmhouse kitchen. Though Antoine was hungry, he found it hard to eat. Gabrielle sat silently watching sparks from the campfire snap toward the first stars of night. When the blue sheet of dusk was finally upon them, Monsieur Vincent came from the coach. He put a hand on Gabrielle's shoulder. "Your father is alert, child. He asks to see you."

A glow brighter than the fire's filled her face. "Oh, Antoine!" she said trembling. "God is answering my prayer! Come with me."

Antoine hesitated, but Monsieur Vincent encouraged him to follow. The priest carried a candle so that Gabrielle could see her father's face when she climbed into the coach. "Oh, Papa. I love you so much." She spoke softly but Antoine could hear outside the door.

"And I love you," Thomas whispered back. "God is good. He provided care for me. . . . On Monsieur Girard's land . . . injured peasants . . . are left to die."

Gabrielle came outside and stopped in front of the priest. "My father is alive because you spoke up for him," she said with emotion. "Monsieur, to show my thanks I will be your servant forever."

Monsieur Vincent touched her hand. "Serve God to show your thankfulness to him—not to me." He smiled. "Now let Antoine take you to the farmhouse. Your father needs much rest. I will stay here."

Antoine had just said good night to Gabrielle at the door when his mother came to him with an iron kettle in her hand. "What will you do about your dreams tonight?" she asked with concern. "Mercure expects that you will sleep with the men by the fire."

Antoine looked up at the dark sky. It crossed his mind to ask God what he should do. Closing his eyes, he breathed a silent prayer. "I will stay out here," he announced. "Two nights ago, you were right. God heard your prayer."

"You did not dream!" She squeezed his hand. "God is at work in all of us! It is almost too good to believe!"

His need for sleep came upon him as soon as Antoine wrapped himself in his cloak by the fire. But before he lay down, he knelt to pray. "Lord of constant mercy, keep watch around me as I sleep. . . ," he began hesitantly.

"You're not praying, are you?" Mercure sat down beside him on his own cloak.

Antoine fell back onto his heels, nodding timidly.

"Hah, well, never do that in the company of pages or guards. Go to church to please the de Gondis and the

Bishop of Paris, of course. But do not practice so much religion that you start looking like a priest!"

Antoine bit his lip.

"Thomas Martel's too sick to go anywhere tonight, so I'm getting some sleep," the guard said wearily. Then without another word he stretched out on the ground. Cautiously Antoine rose to his knees and finished his prayer. As soon as his head was on the blanket, he was asleep.

The fire that glowed around Antoine blazed brighter than any campfire. His eyes watered in the heat of it as he clung to a lone board bobbing in the cold black water. The *Hirondelle* was burning! And Turk Rodomonte's galley was slipping away to freedom—*with Luc on board*—while his father's ship went up in smoke.

Tasting tears, Antoine suddenly sat up. Immediately he looked at Mercure, but the man was snoring loudly. He pulled his cloak around his neck to chase off the cold night air. "Why, God, did you let me dream?" he muttered before putting his head down again. Then he saw Monsieur Vincent standing outside the ring of firelight, watching him.

"I came over to get some rest," he said. "Madame de Gondi is with Thomas now." He crouched down beside Antoine. "But you've had another dream, haven't you? Was it like the one at Villepreux?"

Antoine hung his head. "No, not exactly . . . I prayed I would not dream at all, but God did not answer my prayer."

"How can you be sure of that?" Monsieur Vincent asked. "Perhaps he wanted you to have this dream, so that he could work something good from it."

"Like what!" Antoine huffed.

The priest shrugged. "That depends on the reasons for your dreams. Maybe you should tell me about them."

"I cannot." Antoine put his head into his hand. "Father does not want me to tell anyone about them." He hesitated. "But I would be giving away no secrets if I asked you to pray for Luc, my older brother. We were so close in Romarin, but now he is far . . . far away."

"And you cannot tell me where he is?"

"No, Monsieur, Father would not like it."

"But you worry about him? Is he in danger?"

"Oh, yes, he is. And in misery, too, of the sort I see with Father's men—" He put a finger to his lips, realizing how much he had said.

Monsieur Vincent tapped Antoine's knee. "I have a secret, too, my son. But I will tell it to you because I think it will help you trust God to care for all your needs—and those of your brother who is far away." The priest leaned close to the fire as he pulled back his collar. "What do you see on my neck, Antoine?"

"Why, a line of scars, Monsieur! What are they from?"

The priest rolled up his sleeve. "And here?"

"A thick white scar!"

"Antoine, ten years ago I was captured by pirates. I was shot and then put into the same kind of chains your father's men wear now."

"This happened to you!"

The priest nodded. "On the African coast, I was stripped of every human dignity and sold as a slave. But through this experience, I learned that God in his grace never abandons those who keep their eyes on him. Even as I dug ditches in the desert sun, he put songs into my heart and words of scripture into my mind. And do you know, God's faithfulness began to change the lives of those around me? Eventually, my master chose to believe in Jesus Christ, too. Both of us risked death to escape the Barbary Coast."

"That is an amazing story." Antoine sighed. "Monsieur, your life changes everyone's life—wherever you go."

The priest smiled. "That is the rule in life, not the exception. The scriptures teach us that we will reap what we sow. I encourage you to pray for Luc. As you come to believe that God can work even in bad times, you will have less trouble with dreams."

Antoine managed a smile as he bent on his knees. "Is there a prayer that you could say for him now?"

"Of course."

Mercure stirred just then, but Antoine did not move as Monsieur Vincent began to speak. "O God, the author and lover of peace—to know you is to live—to serve you is to reign. Shield your people from danger, so that all of us who trust in your protection may fear no foe. Through our Lord we pray. Amen."

The priest spread his own cloak near the fire, and soon both of them were asleep.

When Antoine awoke in the morning, he was not even surprised that he had not dreamed again. The peace born in the middle of his being last night was as real to him as the clear sun of the new day. But Mercure Sabre soon came to break the calm with an announcement. "We're traveling after breakfast. The ferryman expects our coach to cross within the hour."

"No!" Antoine protested. "It is too soon."

But Monsieur Vincent was there to put a firm hand on his shoulder. "This time we must obey Mercure, but I have asked him to let us travel very slowly."

"We will do what we have to do," Mercure said to everyone. "We promised to return the man if he survived. Now we are going to do just that. The general cannot be more than four or five leagues ahead of us. We can easily catch up with him by nightfall."

The day proved Mercure Sabre right. Though the jolting carriage was agony to Thomas Martel, the man was still conscious when they entered the prisoners' camp at dusk. After a late-night talk, General de Gondi agreed to let all of them continue on with the march to Marseille. Mercure would guard the coach; Monsieur Vincent, the women, and Gabrielle would tend the sick—including Thomas; and Antoine would learn how to supervise a chain of men.

Within a few days, however, Antoine found himself drawn completely to helping Monsieur Vincent. With the women and Gabrielle, he salved the neck wounds caused by the rough iron collars and changed bandages on dirty, blistered feet. Every night, from the time they made camp until well after dark, he fed prisoners who were too tired to feed themselves.

Only after this was done, did he allow himself the simple pleasure of brushing and rubbing down Jonquille. As the misery of the men increased around him, he found himself slipping away more often to spend time alone with his beautiful horse.

For twenty-eight days they continued their slow journey south on a series of rough roads and crowded river barges. Still the day they dreaded came too quickly. One hot bright morning the conductors ordered the men to halt. They had reached the gates of Marseille.

Guards from the city came to look over the chains of prisoners. Gabrielle ran up to Antoine with tears on her cheeks. "Where is Monsieur Vincent? I just found out that they are bringing chains for Father."

When the priest heard Gabrielle's news, he hurried with them to the coach. He opened the door and helped Thomas out into the strong sunlight. His left arm hung useless as he reached to hug his daughter. Gabrielle clung to him while Monsieur Vincent spoke. "We have talked about this day many times, Thomas, and now it has come."

The man nodded. "I am ready, Father." His eyes grew damp. "I remember the words from Saint Paul that you said so often. 'The man who was a slave when he was called by the Lord is now the Lord's freedman. And the man who was free when the Lord called him is now Christ's slave. You all—slave or free—were bought with a price, that of Christ's own blood. So, serve him, and do not become the slaves of anything or anyone but him."

Monsieur Vincent's eyes were wet, too. "You have quoted well for us, Thomas. God desires wholehearted obedience from all of us."

A few moments later the priest pulled Gabrielle to himself. Thomas stood in silence while a turnkey from the city locked the chain around his neck. As her father was led away, the girl's face crinkled with tears. Monsieur Vincent bent down to look her straight in the eye. "The general tells me that your father will probably be kept on an old galley moored at the east end of the wharf. Madame de Gondi and Antoine's mother are going to take you there by coach. Be encouraged, my child, you will see him again."

"Can't you come, too, Father?" Gabrielle asked.

"I will as soon as I can. Today, however, the general wants me to review Comte de Romarin's fleet with him. Hopefully I will learn things that can help me organize priests and volunteers to ease the hardships of oarsmen."

"Then how about you, Antoine?" Gabrielle said. "Will you go with me?"

"No, he will not!" The strong voice belonged to Antoine's father. "You have played servant long enough, Antoine. Now you must return to being a nobleman's son. As soon as the general secures lodging for us in the city, I am taking you down to the galleys to meet the captains."

Stung by his father's words, Antoine rode into the middle of Marseille with the men. There the general introduced them to a friend of his, a wealthy Florentine jeweler, who was happy to offer them rooms while they were in Marseille. Because they would be on the water most of the day, he suggested that they put their horses in his stable where they would be safe from thieves. And because he was a man with an eye for fine horses as well as jewels, he came out to look at Jonquille more closely after seeing her from the doorway of his shop.

"How can this horse belong to you, lad?" he asked, stopping Antoine as he started to climb back into the saddle.

The general smiled. "Of course you would like that mount, friend. It once belonged to Louis the Just himself."

The man touched Jonquille's nose. "This horse would be worth a small fortune in Marseille."

Antoine's father laughed. "My son would part with his skin before he'd give up that mare."

"I understand that feeling," the jeweler said. "I am glad she will be safe in my stable."

Once the horses had been turned over to the grooms, Mercure excused himself to explore the town. The general then led Antoine, his father, and the priest down to the waterfront. The comte immediately spotted his white *Royale* tied up along the wharf. Like the red galleys to her right and left, Comte de Romarin's flagship had two tall masts and long thin oars that stuck out on each side above the water. Antoine could almost imagine the vessels as strange, wild seabirds stretching their wings before flight.

Anxiety burned a pit into Antoine's stomach when his father motioned them to board the *Royale*. The rocking boat, the chatter of crewmen, and the smell of the sea took him back to the moment when he had boarded the *Hirondelle*.

Behind him on the wharf, Monsieur Vincent squeezed his elbow. "Are you fearful?" he whispered.

"A little," Antoine admitted softly. "Since spring I've hoped that I would never go to sea again."

"Come on!" his father shouted impatiently from the deck. "The captain's just given me word that a pirate ship opened fire on two French galleys heading into port. We're going to rescue whatever survivors there are. You'll see a demonstration of rowing power that you won't soon forget!"

"I can't go!" Antoine said between clenched teeth.

"Pray for strength, Antoine," the priest encouraged him. "Your father wants you on board."

With Monsieur Vincent's help Antoine made it to the narrow upper deck that went around the hull of the galley. A whistle sounded. Hundreds of almost naked, bareheaded men rose with one action to the grab the handles nailed to the great oars in front of them. Back and forth the oarsmen rocked, seven in each row, and the boat began to move.

With shaking knees Antoine followed Monsieur Vincent up the few steps to the small raised poop deck. As soon as they were there, the captain put them to the task of tearing bandages from the cot sheets on board. They had hardly finished the work when Antoine caught a glimpse of the two French galleys broken by cannonfire. The attacking pirate ship was gone, but Antoine wondered if any wounded renegades would be found at sea.

Monsieur Vincent called Antoine to pray with him. Then they hurried among the sweating, bare-chested rowers. The priest pointed to a small open kitchen area where officers were dumping the limp, soaked bodies of rescued men. "Work with me," he urged. "Use the bandages to stop the bleeding."

Antoine bound the slashes on the first half-conscious French officer he came to. Then he began again with the next man who was slumped against the first. His arms trembled, and he felt he must rest. Instead he reached for the next man on the floor. Antoine knelt and rolled him over. When he looked down, a scream of terror came from the depths of his own lungs.

"It's Turk Rodomonte!" he cried, crawling away.

"What's wrong?" Monsieur Vincent grabbed his arm.

Antoine would not look back. "The man there. He is the pirate who threatened my life and captured my brother," he said without thinking.

"He cannot breathe," the priest said tensely. "Help me raise his shoulders up."

Antoine's hands froze behind his back.

"Help me now!" Monsieur Vincent shouted.

Antoine forced himself back to the man. He put his hands under Turk Rodomonte's wet armpits and pulled him up as the priest instructed him. Suddenly the injured man gasped in pain, sucking in a great, wheezing breath of air.

"This man was sick before someone's sword pierced his side," the priest concluded. "I have seen the breath fail in other poor souls who have had their faces destroyed like this. Antoine . . . we must keep his shoulders high so he can breathe."

As they pulled him to the galley's edge and propped him along the wall, the man's eyes rolled like white marbles looking up into Monsieur Vincent's face. "Priest!

Priest!" he gasped. "Don't let me die. I can't get air."

Monsieur Vincent ripped his shirt to check his shallow wound. As he did a small gold crucifix fell from the pirate's neck into his hand.

"How can this be?" Antoine cried. "A Turk who wears the cross of Jesus!"

"I . . . am . . . no Turk," the man struggled as the priest bound his wound. "My name . . . is Alain Douville . . . son of a French nobleman." The man clenched his teeth. "Father! I am afraid to die!"

"Do you believe in the Christ whose cross you wear?" the priest asked. "If you do, you have no reason to fear—"

"God will send me to hell!" The man clutched his chest. "For thirteen years, I have been Turk Rodomonte . . . who kills . . . and steals and . . ." Lack of breath forced him to stop.

Monsieur Vincent took his hand. "God hears your confession. He forgives you because Jesus Christ died for you—no matter what you've done."

The man reached for the small cross in the priest's hand. When he had it, he pressed it against his forehead. "Oh, God, please. . . ," he moaned. "Forgive me!"

Antoine stood in wide-eyed silence as Monsieur Vincent spoke the words of absolution to him. When the priest had finished, the man began gasping in long, hard breaths again. But this time Antoine saw that his struggle was just physical. Prayer had removed his fear.

"Stay with him," the priest said suddenly. "I must speak with the other survivors. But call me at once if he stops breathing again."

Antoine knelt, careful to avoid the man's half-opened eyes. He made himself look at the awful face, and though it had been the terror of his dreams, he felt a hard, dark sadness now. He wondered about Luc. *Did the man even remember that one evil deed from among the many he had done?*

Suddenly the shadow of a sword passed over Alain Douville's ruined face. Antoine saw the man's eyes grow wide with terror. When he looked up, he saw his father with an outstretched blade in his hand. "Don't you know who this is?" his father roared. "I will kill him now because the gallows in Marseille are too good for him."

"Monsieur! Quick!" Antoine screamed, forcing his hands across Alain Douville's chest and neck.

Monsieur Vincent was there in an instant with his hand around the comte's wrist.

"This man took my son!" His father raged. "He burned my ship and killed my men. He deserves to die!"

"Not from your fit of rage," the priest said firmly. "General de Gondi must decide what punishment he deserves."

Trembling, his father lowered the sword. Antoine was about to let his hands slip from the injured man, when Alain Douville's rough fingers touched his arm. "I know you!" he said, searching Antoine's face. "*You* were the young lad . . . on the *Hirondelle* that night."

"Yes." Antoine nodded stiffly. "You never knew, but I—I am Comte de Romarin's younger son."

"And you save me now?" The man put the small crucifix to his chest.

Antoine, unable to explain his feelings, stood up beside Monsieur Vincent. He avoided his father's stare.

The man looked up at him. "Boy, your brother is safe. Know that. I have done much wrong. But for some reason . . . I could not hurt him. He is in Tunis. I have him as a servant . . . in my house."

"Did you hear that, Father?" Antoine said, suddenly in tears. "Luc is alive. Luc is safe."

"I can write . . . Give me paper," Douville said weakly. "I will sign my name to a letter that can set him free even if I die."

Comte de Romarin sheathed his sword as Monsieur de Gondi joined them. "What is going on?" the general asked.

"Monsieur de Gondi . . . do you remember me?" the man on the galley floor gasped. "You taught me . . . to use the sword."

The general dropped to his knees, studying the hideous face. "Monsieur Douville!" His voice trembled. "I thought you died years ago! *Who did this to you?*"

"I did." Antoine's father closed his eyes. "Young Alain Douville was a student officer on my galley fourteen years ago. The crew came back drunk one night. I grabbed the nearest man and made an example of him with my sword."

"Monsieur de Gondi, I was not in the wrong. I stayed my post. I did not leave." The man paused.

The general knit his eyebrows. "Joseph, you never told me any of this. You made this innocent man suffer?"

Antoine's father nodded. "I did. When I woke up

113

from my rage, I knew I would lose everything if you found out. So. . . ," he swallowed several times. "I paid a spice merchant to sell Monsieur Douville in the African slave markets. I thought I would never hear of him again."

The general looked down at the exhausted man. "Instead, my friend, you came back to plague all French merchants as the dreaded Turk Rodomonte."

"Yes, that is exactly what happened. Because of my hatred . . . for Comte de Romarin."

The young captain of the *Royale* came to them. "Excuse me, General, but we are ready to unload the prisoners and injured Frenchmen. I'll send a guard for this ugly Turk."

"Don't touch him. He's a French nobleman," the general replied. "Send for my coach and take him to a good doctor for his wound."

"The man is hideous!" the captain whispered. "Do you think it is a favor to save his life?"

"Quiet!" the general shouted. "You don't know the price this man has paid for his days as a pirate. I am going to do everything in my power to see that he goes free." He scowled at Antoine's father. "But you, Joseph de Romarin? I am close to locking you in the galleys."

"No!" Monsieur Douville protested as he sought out Monsieur Vincent's eyes. "If it can be said that Christ died for my crimes, let the comte know this forgiveness, too." He paused to rest. "I am weary of hate . . . I am so weary of hate."

10

THE TRADE

The next afternoon Mercure Sabre found Antoine brushing Jonquille in the jeweler's stable. "I'm glad to see you here," he said. "We have less than a week to get back to Paris to take up our new assignments. That means we must make a hard, fast ride home—starting today."

Antoine stopped the brush on his mare's tight flank. "I want to go to Romarin, not Paris. After everything I've seen at court and on the galleys, I have no desire to be a nobleman." Antoine started brushing again.

"I travel with you, or without you." The guard turned on his heel. "But I leave today."

As Mercure walked out the door, Antoine buried his face in Jonquille's mane. After a while he bridled and saddled the mare and led her outside. He had his foot in the stirrup ready to mount when he heard Gabrielle's voice.

"Where are you going?"

"Riding!" he snapped. "What does it matter to you?"

He saw her look down across the satin dress she wore. It was almost long enough to hide her new shoes.

"I was hoping you might take this basket of food to my father. You see, things haven't worked out as Monsieur Vincent planned. The old guard there wouldn't let me on the galley—*because I am a girl*."

"Let the priest help you," Antoine said coldly.

"He and the general are looking at sites for a hospital for oarsmen," she replied. "They will be busy most of the day." She studied him as he climbed into the saddle. "What's wrong, Antoine? It's unlike you to be this way."

"You've heard about my father?"

"Well . . . a little." She shifted the basket from one hand to the other. "I know he is very sorry for what he has done. Monsieur Douville told me that even though he forgives the comte, it might take your father a long time to forgive himself."

"You spoke with Monsieur Douville?" Antoine's eyes widened in surprise.

"Monsieur Vincent took me to visit him," she explained. "His face does look terrible, but you should hear the wonderful things he says. He's thinking of dedicating the rest of his life to God—as a priest like Monsieur Vincent himself!"

"He is?" Suddenly Antoine felt less gloomy.

"Yes, he thinks he could work with galley slaves as Monsieur Vincent has been praying some men will do. Because many galley slaves have lost ears and noses to other captains, he thinks they might listen to what he has to say."

116

Antoine reached down for Gabrielle's basket. "Ride to the wharf with me," he said. "I will go to see your father."

Suddenly she seemed shy. "I would like to, but I cannot ride in the new clothes Madame de Gondi bought for me. Will you tell Father about the dress?"

"Yes, of course," Antoine smiled at her. "I'll say you look very nice in it." Then he kicked Jonquille and headed for the wharf.

At the old galley he tied his mare to a post. A young guard with freckles on his nose gave him permission to come on board. The heavy tarpaulins that roofed the galley at night had been pulled to one side. Row after row of ill and injured men drooped side by side on the wooden benches. Because each prisoner had his head shaved and wore identical linen shorts, Antoine had to walk up and down the foul-smelling boat several times before he found Thomas.

Antoine forced himself to smile as he put the basket into Thomas's good hand. "I came to bring a gift from Gabrielle," he explained. "She wants to be here, but girls aren't allowed on board."

"So I've heard." The man returned his smile as he reached for the basket with his good hand. "Give her my thanks." He struggled to go on. "I truly hoped to speak with her again. Everything happened so quickly outside the city gate."

The young freckle-faced guard came close to listen to their conversation. Antoine scowled at his intrusion, but Thomas shook his head.

"Anger won't change anything," he said. "Do you

remember what Monsieur Vincent told us on the march?
If Christ sets you free, you are free indeed. Somehow
God will help me. Monsieur hopes to visit me from time
to time, and I feel blessed knowing Madame de Gondi
will find a good home for Gabrielle until I'm free."

Antoine's throat seemed too full for him to speak.
"Madame bought her a dress. She looks pretty in it."

"I'm sure she does." Thomas looked toward the sky.
"I hope she doesn't change too much in three years."

The guard near them cracked an almond between his
teeth. "So it's your pert, red-haired daughter who keeps
trying to get on board," he said. "The regular guards
warned me about her."

Thomas's cheek twitched as he nodded.

"Look back there." The guard laughed as he pointed
to the wharf behind them. "She's here again. I have half
a mind to let her see you, since I'm the only one on
duty."

"Would you?" Thomas almost rose to his feet.

"For a few minutes, why not?" He walked to the back
of the boat.

Soon Gabrielle was in her father's arms.

"What was this man's crime?" the young guard asked
Antoine as they moved aside to give father and daughter
some time alone.

"He held his master's horse while the man tried to kill
the king." Antoine's voice was tight with anger.
"Thomas Martel was punished just because he obeyed
his master's order. He knew nothing of the nobleman's
plan."

The guard wet his lips. "He will never row. Look at

his arm. Now the king has the worthless expense of feeding him. Have you thought of trying to get him freed?"

"Freed?" Antoine said the word so loudly that Gabrielle and her father turned their heads.

"I might be able to convince the chief guard of it in exchange for 1500 livres." The man with freckles grinned.

Gabrielle gasped. "Madame de Gondi or even your parents, Antoine, have that kind of money!"

But Thomas took her by the shoulder. "Don't you ask them for one coin," he warned. "The general and the comte see family men go into chains every year. They cannot be expected to pay for the freedom of one man."

Gabrielle dropped her eyes. "But we don't have one sou between us, Father."

The guard spoke again. "It takes money, because some poor soul must be bought to take your father's place. He could be a rower or an invalid like yourself, man, but we must have another body on that bench so that no one is missing in the count."

Thomas studied his injured arm. "I suppose you are stuck with me. I have no money, and no one would want to take my place."

Suddenly Antoine's head started aching with a wonderful, yet terrible idea. "I think I have a way to get the money," he said abruptly.

Gabrielle rushed to him. "How?"

Antoine hurried off the old vessel without answering her. He freed Jonquille's reins.

"Wait for me!" Gabrielle cried, catching up to him.

Because she was beside him, Antoine led his horse. He

walked quickly, fearing he would lose the courage he needed to carry out his plan. Finally they were back at the jeweler's house and shop. He left Jonquille in Gabrielle's care and rushed inside.

"Monsieur!" he said to the jeweler with little breath left. "Would you like to buy my mare?"

The man looked up from the fine gold chain in his hand. "What! Your father said you'd sell it to no one!"

"I have something in Marseille that I want more than my horse."

Gabrielle suddenly was at his elbow. "Antoine! Don't do this! Jonquille means everything to you!"

He shook her off. "Fifteen hundred livres, and the mare is yours."

"Are you sure you want to do this? Is your horse still as sound as she was when I saw her yesterday?"

"She is," Antoine said impatiently. "If you don't believe me, look outside. I have her at your door."

"Then I will buy her." The man smiled. "Let me put the money into a pouch—before you regain your senses."

As the coins clinked together, Antoine held his breath. Mercure Sabre walked through the door. "Antoine, I see you have Jonquille saddled," he said. "I trust this means you are riding to Paris with me."

"I am selling my horse to free Thomas Martel from the galley," Antoine said quickly. He pressed his lips together as the jeweler closed the money bag.

Mercure Sabre jumped in front of Antoine, taking the pouch before it could reach his hand.

"No, he cannot do that!" Mercure raged. "You fool, Antoine. You know the horse belongs to the king."

"No, she's mine!" Antoine shouted back. "I can sell her if I want to."

The jeweler looked at both of them and took the money. "I see I was too hasty in this."

"Please, buy my horse!" Antoine pleaded. "If you do not take her, I have nothing else to exchange for the life of this girl's father."

The jeweler looked at him with sympathy. "Well . . . there is something else. If you want to save your horse, ask your guard friend here to sell the diamond clasp on his hat. I have been eyeing it since the moment I met him, and I would pay him well over the amount you need."

"Mercure! What do you say?" Antoine bit his lip.

"Are you an imbecile?" Mercure looked down his nose at Gabrielle. "We discussed this in the marketplace days ago. I have no interest in helping peasants, even well-dressed ones, and I never will!"

Gabrielle's chin went to her chest, and she ran outside. Antoine followed her, trembling with rage at Mercure. "I am sorry," he said. "You hear so many harsh words."

She looked at him, her eyes completely dry. "Before I met Madame de Gondi, your mother, and you, I expected all rich people to act just as Mercure Sabre does now. For that reason, I think, I am even less disappointed than you that your idea didn't work. But Antoine . . . thank you. Thank you for even thinking of selling Jonquille. I know how much you treasure her."

Antoine clenched his fists. "I wish there was a way.

I'm sure your father's hopes are up. Now I have to go back to tell him I have failed."

"But he will be proud of you for trying." She smiled. "It was so good to hope about his freedom, even for a moment. Could we walk around the city a little while, so you will not have to tell him the bad news right away?"

Antoine nodded. He let Gabrielle lead Jonquille as they went through the busy streets. "Mercure Sabre wants me to leave for Paris today," he said hesitantly when they had walked for a while. "I am to live in the palace to serve the king. I know Father wants me to go back, but I don't want the selfish, boastful life of a nobleman."

She looked at him. "Can't you go back, and just be the same kind of person you are now? Just think, if you and the de Gondis hadn't helped me, where would I be now? Antoine, God can give you the courage to serve him, even in the king's palace."

Antoine liked the sparkle in her eyes. "You think I should go back?"

She smiled. "I will miss you," she said looking down at her dress. "When my father is released I will live the peasant's life again. But, you, Antoine, have the chance to be a nobleman." Her gray eyes were serious, yet bright. "I know God loves us both the same, but I think he's putting us into two different worlds . . . He's like a good master who knows where and how we can serve him best."

Antoine dropped back to rub his hand along Jonquille's neck. "Until now I was thinking mostly of what

I wanted to do. But I think you're right. God may want me back at the palace. The day the king gave this horse to me, I promised him that I would not grow selfish. Yet, I have been thinking only of what I want to do."

"Then you'd better find Mercure before he leaves," Gabrielle said, looking at the deep shadows in the street.

Antoine nodded. "But first I must speak with your father. Please, take Jonquille back to the jeweler's stable. Look for Mercure's black charger and if the guard comes for his horse, tell him I want to meet him there."

While Gabrielle turned Jonquille around, Antoine sprinted toward the wharf. It was the old guard who eyed him and reluctantly gave permission for him to go on board. In preparation for night, the tarpaulins had already been drawn as a roof over the prisoners' heads. Antoine's eyes had trouble adjusting to the dim gray light under the canvas until he came to Thomas Martel's place.

"Thomas, wake up. There is something I must tell you," he said unhappily to the prisoner who dozed with his chin resting on his chest. The man stirred, and when he looked up, Antoine saw the face of *Alain Douville*!

"Monsieur!" he cried. "What are you doing here!"

Monsieur Douville seemed shocked to see him, too. "Thomas became a free man this afternoon. I thought you would know by now!"

"How? He had no money—"

"I became his substitute," Monsieur Douville's awful face warmed with a slow smile. "After all the wrong I've done, God gave me something good to do. . . . Thomas has a daughter who needs him and by God's grace I am well enough to take his place."

"But you were to be freed!" Antoine exclaimed. "The general said so."

"I *am* free," the man said calmly. "That is why I am here. I know Christ died for me. Now I choose to take the place of Thomas Martel, my brother in the faith."

Antoine gazed at him with disbelief.

"Antoine, for fourteen years I died inside each time someone stared at me as you are doing now." His voice cracked. "But now I am not ashamed of what I can be with the help of God."

A lump formed in Antoine's throat. "You were the terror of my dreams, but now, Monsieur, I have nothing but respect for you."

"Ahh . . . but if that old sailor hadn't grabbed the torch to set the *Hirondelle* afire, I would have blinded *you*! Can you be so quick to forgive?"

Antoine trembled. "That is in the past. Your forgiveness has kept my father from ruin, and now you have traded your freedom for that of Thomas Martel. It is not so hard to be grateful to you."

Monsieur Douville lifted his head. "I need to thank you, too. I know you recognized me straightaway when I was pulled from the water. Yet you saved me from a horrid death. You showed me forgiveness first. That is why I survived long enough to forgive."

Antoine shook his head. "It is Monsieur Vincent who must be thanked. He's the one who helped me change my heart."

Monsieur Douville nodded. "And he is the one who first told me about Thomas and Gabrielle. Our friend Monsieur Vincent is an extraordinary man. From one faithful life look how many good things have come."

Monsieur Douville's words stayed with Antoine even when he stepped off the dark galley and hurried toward the jeweler's stable. As the building came into view, he realized that Mercure Sabre had both horses outside, readied for the journey. He paused on the cobblestones. For a moment he felt it would be too great a challenge to ride to Paris while his family and closest friends stayed behind.

But then he saw Monsieur Vincent starting down the street to meet him. The priest's face wrinkled with its familiar grin as he walked to Antoine's side. "I hear you're going back to Paris," he said enthusiastically.

Suddenly Antoine was sure there was purpose in his going. He would serve the King of France faithfully. Perhaps someday, God would allow him to tell Louis the Thirteenth about the best friendship of all—with the King of Kings himself.

Historical Note

Vincent de Paul lived in seventeenth-century France, an age made famous by such well-known stories as *The Three Musketeers* and *Cinderella*. Though many of the characters in *The King's Reward* are imaginary, they reflect the kinds of people—from galley slaves to the king—whose lives were changed by this French priest.

For young Vincent de Paul a career in the church provided an escape from the poverty of his peasant home. Several experiences, including two years of slavery on the Barbary Coast, deepened his dedication to the priesthood. Eventually he did much to reform the Roman Catholic Church in France by training other priests and setting an example of faith and service. Nine years after his ordination, his work of distributing alms from the royal family made him the friend of both wealthy courtiers and poor outcasts.

In 1613 he began serving the General of the Royal Galleys Philipe-Emmanuel de Gondi, first as a tutor for his sons and then as a chaplain for his family and tenants. The de Gondis gave Monsieur Vincent time to preach in rural areas. He organized small groups of Christian men and women to help their needy neighbors. When Monsieur Vincent saw the horrible conditions of galley prisoners, he obtained a house where convicts could receive rest and nourishment. He traveled to Marseille to start a hospital for oarsmen. Soon King Louis the Thirteenth made Monsieur Vincent the Chaplain General of Galleys. Under the priest's direction, other compassionate men and women provided health care, spiritual instruction, and a postal service for galley prisoners.

In 1625 Monsieur Vincent founded the Congregation of the Mission for the purpose of preaching to the poor. Later the institute of the Daughters of Charity was formed when a small group of unmarried women, inspired by Monsieur Vincent's dedication, committed themselves to serving the outcasts of Paris. The workers in these organizations eventually improved living conditions for thousands of poor people in France.

But Monsieur Vincent's commitment to charity did not blind him to the fact that the wealthy also need the Savior's love. In 1643 the priest was called to the bedside of France's dying king. Because of Monsieur Vincent's counsel, Louis the Thirteenth died speaking the name of Jesus Christ.

Three hundred years after Vincent de Paul's own death in 1660, there are approximately 4,000 Vincentian priests and 43,000 Daughters of Chairty carrying on Monsieur Vincent's work in 64 countries around the world.